Lannigan's West

Old Pat Lannigan had fought long and hard for his Circle Star cattle empire and hated above all else nesters and cattle combines. But now one of his sons was going to be a farmer and the M.L.G. Cattle Combine was building a huge new ranch. Worse still that ranch was going up on Circle Star land – which Pat hadn't registered.

A range war seemed inevitable and indeed the shooting soon started. Cold-blooded murder and bushwhacking became the order of the day and feeble Sheriff Walt Eckerton just wasn't up to solving any murder.

Only Jim Lannigan, with his sharp brain and formidable skills with fist and gun, had a hope of bringing peace to the range. Battered and bloodied though he might be, sheer determination would see him through – if a bullet didn't get to him first.

Lannigan's West

Jake Ross

A Black Horse Western

ROBERT HALE · LONDON

ISBN 0 7090 7266 X

Robert Hale Limited
Clerkenwell House
Clerkenwell Green
London EC1R 0HT

Typeset by
Derek Doyle & Associates, Liverpool.
Printed and bound in Great Britain by
Antony Rowe Limited, Wiltshire.

CHAPTER ONE

'Who are you to tell me what tuh do an' what not tuh do?' said Clem Lannigan. His face was pale beneath its tan, his eyes blazed, his whole tall, slender body trembled. 'Bessie don't want to live here with the rest o' the bunch an' neither do I. We want tuh live our own life in our own home. Surely we can do that without . . .'

'An' be a sneakin' little 'nester',' sneered old Pat Lannigan. His voice was thick with passion. To him home-steaders, 'nesters', were the lowest things that crawled.

'You want to be a dictator,' said Clem. 'You want everybody to live like you, think like you, do as you say. You won't give any body a chance. You'd do anythin' to keep this empire of yours, wouldn't you? Lord of creation – But I'm not scared of yuh – or your dirty-fighting men. An' there'll be others. There'll be . . .'

His father's huge horny fist flush in the mouth cut off the rest of the sentence. He staggered back against the kitchen table, his eyes dazed, his burst lips spilling blood.

Old Pat had put all the weight of his huge arms and heavy body behind that blow. He marvelled that his son was not unconscious. He felt no qualms, and, if he felt any admiration, quickly stifled that. He stood over his twenty-three year old son with his huge clenched fists hanging at his sides and said:

'Get out of here. Marry your Bessie. Become a stinking,

5

muck-scratching nester. An' don't let me see hide nor hair o' yuh again.'

Clem shook his head feebly, wiped the back of his hand across his mouth, looked at the red-stained hand curiously. He pushed himself slowly away from the table. It was as if his Dad wasn't there any more. Slowly he crossed the kitchen floor to the door. It flew open as he reached it and his younger brother, Jim, almost collided with him. Though only twenty, Jim was bigger than Clem, he promised to have the Herculean frame of his father. He stood still in the door way and looked from one to the other. When he spoke he was looking at his Dad. There was no hatred, only a cold disregard.

He said, 'What've yuh done to Clem?'

It was Clem himself who answered. 'Never mind, Jim, I'm going now. I ain't comin' back.' He brushed past his brother. Jim turned as if to detain him, then, with a gesture of resignation, let him go.

He turned to his Dad. 'I thought it'd come to this,' he said coldly. His face was expressionless. He wasn't fiery like Clem, but for that matter, all the more dangerous.

'Why can't you give a man a chance?' he said.

'It's nuthin' tuh do with you,' growled old Pat. His wrath had subsided.

The middle door swung open and Beulah, his wife, came through. She halted, hands on hips, eyeing her husband and her son, standing apart in tense attitude like contestants.

She was a big, rawboned, masculine woman. Once she had been beautiful, but now her face was lined. Kindness very seldom shone in her blue eyes.

'What's goin' on?' she said.

The two men both started to speak at once.

'Hold your hosses,' she barked . . . 'Pat?'

'I've jest sent Clem packin'.'

'Best thing tuh do,' said Beulah coldly. 'Ungrateful cuss!'

6

'Jim's savage,' continued Pat. 'He thinks I hadn't oughta . . .'

'Nor you hadn't,' interrupted Jim. 'He's your own flesh an' blood. He ain't done any crime.'

'You mind your own business,' his mother rasped. 'We don't want our youngest whippersnapper tellin' us what tuh do. Your Dad and I built this place 'fore you were born. Fought Injuns for it. Sweat, an' toiled, an' fought. We don't want no damn 'nesters' hanging round us. Clem made his own bed . . .'

Jim shrugged, turning away; he had heard so much of it before. He disregarded the rest of his mother's tirade but, as he passed through the door, turned his head and said:

'Some day I'm gonna leave, too.'

'Bull' Kinsell was a drunkard. He'd been so drunk last night that the boys had left him in town, asleep across the table in the Jolly Moses Saloon, and gone on without him. As he rode his lonely morning trail he knew he'd catch hell from old Pat when he got to the Circle Star. But he felt too wretched to care. He'd had some hangovers in his day, but this one was the grand-daddy of 'em all.

He figured he was a couple of miles or so from the Circle Star ranch when he first spotted the buzzards. A bunch of them were circling in the sky to the right of him. Circling above something below that rise. He reined in his horse and watched with bleary eyes. The carrion were squabbling as they wheeled lower. Bull shook his head violently from side to side. His curiosity was beginning to dispel the haze a little. He turned his horse's head and urged the beast in the direction of the disturbance. The buzzards saw him coming and rose a little higher, milling in a hovering bunch and uttering their shrill, horrible cries.

Bull reached the rise and looked down, his head instinctively dropping to the butt of his gun. But it was only a steer that lay in the grass down there. Bull spurred

7

his horse down the slope. He dismounted behind the huge, still bulk of the longhorn. Yes, it was a dead 'un all right. He got down on one knee and looked at the brand.

The familiar ringed star.

Bull cuffed back his Stetson and scratched his head. He couldn't figure that at all. The steer had been shot – right through the brain. He looked more closely. He felt one of its legs that was swollen and misshapen. It was broken. That explained the shooting all right.

But why had the carcase been left there? It was old Pat's express order that anything like that be reported immediately and a wagon fetched from the ranch-house to haul the carcase back there. Evidently this one had not been reported or the carcase would have been removed long since. Judging by the look of it, and the proximity of the buzzards, the steer had been there quite a while. Probably all night. Did that mean the beast had been shot by somebody who didn't belong to the Circle Star?

The fumes of alcohol were fading away from Bull Kinsell's brain and the stagnant lump of grey matter was beginning to work overtime. But Bull had never been extra bright. He rose to his feet and turned to his horse as if he held the solution to the problem. The beast seemed restive, its eyes shifted, its nostrils quivered. It sensed something. Bull turned quickly. Something glinted in the shadow of those rocks over there . . .

As he drew his gun the rifle cracked. The slug hit him in the stomach. He grunted, buckling up, his hand trying to bring the gun up, his mouth spilling curses. Bull Kinsell had never lacked guts. The rifle spoke again. The impact of the slug, in his chest this time, straightened Bull up and spun him around. He fell backwards across the carcase of the steer. His big body jerked twice, then he lay still, spreadeagled, the gun slowly sliding away from uncurling fingers, sliding down the steer's flank and losing itself in the long grass.

Riding slowly with head bent, brows knit in sombre

8

thought, Jim Lannigan heard the shot. He jerked his head up, turned his horse a little with a pressure of his knees, heading him in the direction of the sound. Then he heard the second shot. One shot might mean one of the boys shooting at a rattler or prairie dog. Two might mean the same. But the boys didn't usually waste slugs like that! He set his horse at a gallop.

He was mystified and horrified when the buzzards, now increased in number, led him to the still warm body of 'Bull' Kinsell. A drunkard, but a square shooter for all that – and the older body of the slaughtered steer. Weighing things up, Jim rode at a gallop at the cluster of rocks, only means of ambush thereabouts. His gun was out, ready, and he trusted to luck. But the bushwhacker's nest was empty. All he found were two spent shells and the faint imprints of the knees and toes of a kneeling man. The thick, long grass revealed no footprints or hoof-marks.

Jim retraced his steps. As gently as possible he lifted Bull's heavy body across the front of his saddle. A glint in the deep grass attracted him, and he bent and retrieved Bull's gun. He spun the cylinder, his lips curling savagely at what he saw. He tucked the gun in his belt and, mounting, set off for the Circle Star. He caught up with Bull's horse, its terror now subsided, trotting homewards.

CHAPTER TWO

The air was full of the sounds of many hammers striking wood, the rasping of saws, the cries of men at work: the sounds floating up from the valley to Jim Lannigan sitting motionless on his horse on top of the rise. He pressed his knees to the mare's flanks and gently eased her down the slope. As he reached the level ground a man walked towards him with a sawn-off shotgun in the crook of his arm.

'Hi yuh,' said Jim.

'Hi-yuh,' replied the man, grudgingly friendly.

'My name's Lannigan – Jim Lannigan.'

The man eased the gun slightly forward. His tone was wary. 'You ol' Pat Lannigan's son?'

'Yeh.'

'Your Paw kicked up a ruckus last time he was here.'

'Yeh, I know. Dad's a mite hasty. I didn't come to make any trouble. Jest mebbe to talk to a few o' the men.'

'Wal, you'd better see Mancy Carter, the foreman . . . here he is.'

Jim turned to face the second man, coming across the trampled grass towards them. A man as big as himself, but older by ten years or more, grim, square-faced, with a thread of black moustache above his wide thin lips.

Mancy Carter addressed the shotgun guard. 'Who's this?'

'Jim Lannigan – ol' Pat's son.'

Carter's voice and expression did not change as he turned to Jim and said:

10

'We wouldn't need guards around the place if it weren't for bull-headed cusses like your father . . . What can I do for yuh?'

'In the first place,' said Jim levelly. 'You can keep my father's name out of it. He didn't send me here – an' now that I am here, I don't want to talk about him.'

Something like a smile crossed and disappeared from Carter's grim, blocky visage.

'All right,' he said, 'climb down an' state your business.'

Jim dismounted.

'Might as well come over to the office,' Carter said. 'Dink here 'ull see to your hoss.'

As Jim followed the foreman he heard Dink mutter about bein' a shotgun guard, not a hoss-minder, but he was gratified to note that nevertheless he caught hold of the mare's reins and brought her along behind them.

Carter's office was a ramshackle cabin on a piling of bricks with four wooden steps leading up to the narrow door. The foreman unlocked it, with a key taken from the pocket of his jeans. Jim followed him inside as the guard arrived with his mare and tied her to a stump of hitching-post by the corner of the building. Jim took stock of the dusty interior of the cabin, the roll-top desk, open and scattered with papers, the few nondescript chairs. One of them had a belt, with holstered gun, slung over its back. Jim had wondered at Carter being unarmed. Now he covertly eyed the worn walnut butt of the gun, the belt dark and colourless with sweat. It had been worn for many years, the gun doubtless used many times.

'Sit down, Mr Lannigan,' said Carter affably. He squatted straddle-legged on the chair by the desk, resting his arms on the back and facing Jim. Jim took a seat opposite him by the pot-bellied unlit stove.

'Have a ceegar,' said Carter, taking two from his vest-pocket.

Jim took one, bit the end off and spat it in the cold ashes beneath the stove. The foreman struck a match.

11

They lit up. Carter blew twin jets of smoke down his nostrils. 'Shoot, Mr Lannigan,' he said.

Briefly Jim told him of the murder of 'Bull' Kinsell and the mysterious slaughter of the Circle Star steer.

Carter heard him out without a change of expression. Then he said 'An' so your Paw thinks my men had somethin' tuh do with it.'

'Wal, frankly, yes,' Jim told him 'But, like I told you before, Dad didn't send me here. I jest came tuh see if any of your men had seen or heard anythin' suspicious goin' on that might throw some light on the mystery. Bull was one o' the best; he was my friend . . . but he was a boozer. The boys left him behind in town the night before he was shot. Some of your men must've seen him there. Maybe they got acquainted with him. Maybe they saw him in a fight – or saw him win a bankroll. The motive for the murder might've been robbery. I'm not sayin' any o' your men are mixed up in it – but they might be able to help. *Sabe?*'

For assent the foreman rose to his feet. 'Only about a dozen of the men stayed late in town that night if I remember rightly,' he said. 'I'll see my *segunda*. Maybe he can tell us who they were.'

Jim followed him and they picked their way around piles of bricks and timber and among busily working carpenters, labourers and the rest. Many of them greeted Carter as 'boss'. He stopped and spoke to one grizzled oldtimer who was loading a barrow with bricks. The old man straightened his back and pointed with a horny forefinger.

Following his directions Carter finally accosted a small vicious-looking man in jeans, and a wide-awake that seemed three sizes too large for him.

Carter introduced him as Pete Listery. His hand was cold and claw-like in Jim's, his greeting surly. On hearing the young man's business he became truculent.

'You ain't a lawman are yuh?' he said.

'No.'

'Wal, what's the sheriff doin'? He's the one who oughta be makin' enquiries.'

'The sheriff's outa town,' Jim told him. 'He'll do the necessary when he comes back.'

'Wal, I figure . . .'

Carter interrupted the argument, saying brusquely, 'If you know who went to town that night let's have 'em here.'

'I've got an idea,' muttered Listery. He called a man to him and sent him on the errand.

While they waited in silence Jim rolled himself a cigarette and then offered the 'makings' to the other two. Carter declined in favour of another ceegar, but with a muttered thanks Listery took the stuff and set to work with clumsy fingers. He was no cowhand.

'These the men?' said Carter.

Listery looked up. 'Yeh.'

There were eight of them, at least half of whom were palpable Irish labourers. 'Micks' as old Pat Lannigan would call them.

One in particular towered head and shoulders over the others and had a mop of dirty corn-coloured hair above a huge, sly, square face. He stepped forward in front of the others and said to Carter. 'Ye wanted us, sor?'

'Yes, Callahan,' Carter turned to him. 'Maybe you'd better do the talking.' He faced the men again. 'This is Jim Lannigan from the Circle Star. He'd like tuh ask you a few questions.'

Callahan grinned at Jim, showing a row of huge uneven teeth. Then he turned to his pardners. 'Right, men?'

There were murmurs of assent.

'Shoot, sor,' said Callahan.

Jim was very polite and almost official. 'I gather all you men were in Jumptown on Thursday night.'

'We were,' said Callahan. His companions growled behind him. Callahan's manner was cocky. The rest seemed pretty truculent. They weren't a very prepossessing-looking bunch.

'Did any of you see a drunken cowboy from the Circle Star? A big simple-looking *hombre* called 'Bull' Kinsell.'

'I met 'Bull',' said Callahan. 'We had a drink together.' He seemed mystified now.

Jim reflected that the Circle Star puncher and this big Irishman must've looked quite a pair. In a few blunt phrases he told the men of the mysterious murder of Bull. Callahan was incredulous. The others were not greatly moved. They had only seen Bull knocking around.

Jim said to Callahan. 'Where did Bull go after he left you?'

'He joined a card-school. Me an' the boys went down the street an' left him to it.'

'Did you see him again that night?'

'Yes, we did. When we was leaving town. It was pretty late. We saw him talkin' to another man outside the Jolly Moses.'

The rest of the men backed up Callahan's statement. 'Do you know who the other man was?'

Being strangers in town they didn't.

'What did he look like?'

It was too dark to see properly. He was biggish, maybe middle-aged. After a bit of haggling they decided he either had a beard or a bushy moustache.

It looked like Jim had reached rock bottom as regards Bull Kinsell's depradations in town that fateful night. He asked if any of the men had been out on the range – maybe heard a shot or seen something.

No, nobody had been out on the range – nobody had seen nothin'!

Carter said drily 'We don't like the men to go out on the range. Your Paw might think they were trespassin' with some ulterior motive and take umbrage.'

Jim swallowed a snappy comeback: he had to admit that Carter was right at that!

'Anyway,' continued the foreman. 'None of our men are range-riders. In their spare time they either amuse

14

themselves at the camp here, or go into Jumptown for a night out.'

The 'bhoys' grinned and laughed and, as one man, were jocularly 'right there' with their boss on the last sentence. Jim could not but admit that Mancy Carter had at least co-operated with him.

'Well, thanks anyway,' he said. He bade *adios* to Callahan, Pete Listery and the rest of the boys. He collected his horse and Carter walked to the edge of the camp with him. Before they parted the foreman said:

'I'm sorry I couldn't help yuh more. Accept my condolences on the death of Bull Kinsell an' pass them on to whoever's concerned.'

'Bull had no kin as far as I know,' said Jim. 'Thanks anyway,' he rode away.'

Very smooth. Yes, very smooth.

When the M.L.G. Cattle Combine first began to build this huge new ranch a fortnight ago, old Pat Lannigan nearly had an apopletic fit. He hadn't even heard about it until the wagons unloaded their cargoes, and the men had begun to work. They couldn't do it! He'd show 'em who was who! They weren't going to build on the land he had fought and sweated for – jumped-up city people with their lily-white fingers sending men to take over his territory!

He led a bunch of his men and his six sons, Hannibal, Ep, Jonathan, Kim, Clem and Jim, to the camp of the invaders and forced them at the point of levelled rifles, to stop work. Then he gave them twenty-four hours to pack up and vamoose.

Next morning a posse, led by Walt Eckerton, sheriff of Jumptown, rode up to the Circle Star ranch. With them they brought the M.L.G. Combine's legal representative, J. Woolington Scott, a fiery little New Englander with a bulging portfolio.

Pat ordered them off his grounds. Plump sheriff Walt was sweating with distress. He didn't like doing this. But he

had the law on his side – he had to do it – he'd advised Pat
to calm down and listen.

The old man stood on the verandah with the posse clustered like sheep below him.

'All right,' he said, 'speak your piece.'

J. Woolington Scott kneed his horse to the forefront.
He'd been to a riding academy and knew how to sit a
beast. He wasn't scared of old Pat neither.

He asked to see Mr Lannigan's bill of sale, his rights to
the land. The old man was incredulous and abusive. He'd
fought Injuns and renegades from the desert for it.
Woolington Scott explained gently that taking land by
brute force did not gain ownership . . . then old Pat drew
his gun. Still the little lawyer stood his ground. The
deputies' hands hovered uncertainly over their guns.

'For Pete's sake don't start anythin', Pat,' said Sheriff
Eckerton.

Pat brandished his Colt. 'Get tuh hell out of here,' he
bawled.

'All right,' said the sheriff wearily. 'But I give you fair
warning . . .'

'Git!' screamed Pat.

'C'mon, boys.'

As the posse turned their horses and went, Pat
Lannigan returned to the house. For one of the few times
in his sixty-odd years he was uncertain, even apprehensive.

For a couple of weeks after that he left the M.L.G. camp
alone. His family and his own men felt the brunt of his
savage temper. Clem left and Jim was on the verge of rebel-
lion.

Then 'Bull' Kinsell got shot and right away Pat blamed
the M.L.G. people. Jim had a tough job persuading him
against riding down there with a bunch of men and taking
the place apart. Finally Pat agreed to let him go down and
investigate first himself.

Jim went first to town to call on Walt Eckerton, only to
discover the sheriff was away on business. Consequently,

he had gone to the M.L.G. place on his lonesome.

As he rode back to the Circle Star after his interview with Mancy Carter and his men, Jim's brain was working doubletime. He couldn't quite figure Carter, or his *segunda*, Pete Listery. One moment he told himself they were just a couple of *hombres* doing a job of work for their bosses back East – then he told himself that there seemed something fishy about them – although he couldn't put his finger on what. Maybe it was just his naturally suspicious nature – plus the fact that a pard of his had been brutally murdered.

And that slaughtered steer. How did that fit in the set-up? Maybe it was one of the Circle Star men who'd shot it and forgot to report the incident. And now he'd be too scared to do so. Old Pat had sent men packing for much less than that.

Anyway, how come Bull got shot so close to the steer? That seemed *too* much of a coincidence. Maybe the dead beast had just been used as a decoy. But why pick on Bull – what harm had that big, boozy, good-natured cuss ever done anybody? Maybe in his clumsy way he had bored in where he wasn't wanted. Whoever had done the job hadn't taken any chances.

Jim was deep in thought and his first intimation of danger was a slug whistling under his nose, and the echoing crack of a rifle. His horse reared. Jim instinctively urged him forward and the second shot passed behind them.

Jim rode in a half-circle, turning the horse's head and galloping him full-tilt to the cluster of scrub from behind which the firing had come. He hung low over the horse's neck, his gun levelled. He thought he saw a movement in the shade of the scrub and fired twice. There was no answering shot.

He reached the cover, reining in his horse, throwing himself from it on to his knees, gun still levelled. It was then that for the first time in the stillness he heard hooves

17

retreating. He ran to the other side of the scrub. The rider was well out of range and riding hard. He evidently hadn't wasted much time when he found his bushwhack victim was inclined to be offensive.

Jim frowned, perplexed. But where was this mysterious rider heading? That way didn't lead to the M.L.G. or to town. It led only to the arid, scrubby waste of the fabulous Gila Desert, that strange Arizonian hotbed where only wandering tribes of Indians and scuttling lizards lived.

CHAPTER THREE

As Jim dismounted outside the ranch-house of the Circle Star the house door opened and Abel Cornford came out and across the verandah, and down the steps. Abel was old Pat's foreman and *segunda*. He'd been with him for almost twenty years and understood him perhaps better than anyone except Beulah, his wife. Abel's head was downcast and he didn't see Jim until the younker spoke to him. Jim was surprised to see him there at that time of day. One look at Abel's lined face was enough to start him speculating.

'What's the matter?' he asked.

'There's a coupla dozen head o' cattle missin',' said Abel. 'We've scoured the range and can't find hide nor hair of 'em. We've even been round Old Smoky and into the edge of the Gila.' He shrugged, his forehead wrinkled with worry. 'Nary a sign!'

'What's Dad gotta say about it all?' said Jim.

'He's hopping mad!'

'In that case I'd better leave my news till later on. I'm hungry. I'll go across to the cookhouse an' get some chow. Then I'll come out to yuh. Where are yuh?'

'About half a mile this side Ol' Smoky,' said Abel as he mounted his horse. 'I'll see yuh. *Adios.*'

'*Adios.*'

Jim found the cook, 'Greaseball' Masters, 'Greasy' for short, a perpetually perspiring 14 stone, cooking a midday meal for men who were working in the vicinity and could get back to the ranch for dinner.

Jim helped himself to a generous plateful of stew and poured himself a cup of thick black coffee.

'Greasy', always taciturn, grunted a greeting and continued with his work.

Jim carried his chow to the bunkhouse. Kicking open the loosely-swinging door, he was surprised to find the place already occupied. A man sat on a bunk opposite the door with his head in his hands, yellow hair coming through his fingers. He looked up. 'Howdy, Corny,' said Jim. 'What ails you?'

'Corny' Macintosh was youngish, rather weak-featured. By Circle Star standards he was still a 'new fish' having only been there about twelve months.

He said 'I fell off my hoss. I came here to rest up a bit.'

'No bones busted?'

'Naw. Just a headache. It's clearin' up a bit now. Still, I may as well have chow before I go out again.' He rose to his feet. 'I'll go and get some.'

Jim watched him go curiously. He was a mite unsteady on his feet.

But when Jim turned his head and saw the half-empty whisky bottle underneath the bunk on which Corny had been sitting he understood things better. He crossed the floor and picked the bottle up. He uncorked it. One sniff was enough. It was raw hooch! As he reseated himself and attacked his meal his boyish face wore a very thoughtful expression. He'd never liked Corny overmuch. Still, maybe he was prejudiced.

When the yellow-haired waddy returned with his dinner Jim was mopping-up his plate. He rose, hitching up his gunbelt.

'*Adios.*'

'*Adios,*' said Corny.

As he crossed the yard he passed men on their way to the midday meal.

'Have yuh seen Abel Conford?' he yelled.

20

'He passed us half-an-hour ago heading towards the Gila.'

Evidently Abel was riding back to Old Smoky like he promised.

After about forty minutes hard riding Jim reached the place. Old Smoky was a very deep, sheer-walled dry gulch, a yawning divide between the range and the shimmering heat-haze of the Gila Desert. There was nobody about. Jim was surprised. He looked across the gaping chasm, across to the Gila, a desolate place of sand and rocks, and emaciated scrub. When he was a kid he was scared of the Gila, even now something about it made him shiver.

When his Mom and Dad built the Circle Star they had to fight marauding Indians and border scum, who swooped down on their meagre heads of cattle, running them off and disappearing into the desert from whence they came.

Jim shaded his eyes with his hand, squinting against the sun-glare. The fabulous Gila told him nothing.

He kneed his horse tentatively to the edge of Old Smoky. He looked down. The floor was bare and rocky, clear today. Oft-times you couldn't see the bottom because of the ground mist that billowed there. That's how Old Smoky got it's name.

This huge chasm stretched for almost a mile, a natural boundary for much of Circle Star land. About half a mile to the left of where Jim was now the sides sloped a little, and there a precarious trail had been cut. Maybe the men were along there. Jim turned his horse.

He saw the men before he reached his destination. There was a cluster of them on the lip of Old Smoky where the edge broke and shelved as the tortuous sloping trail began. Jim reined in among them in a small cloud of dust.

'What's goin' on?' he yelled.

They pointed down below.

'There's a steer down there,' said one.

Jim dismounted and walked to the edge with the rest.

21

Far down below, so far that he had a job to recognize them, were Abel Cornford and three of Jim's brothers. They were clustered around a dirty-brown motionless bulk.

'Keep your eyes on my hoss,' said Jim. 'The little cuss is quite capable of followin' me.'

'All right.'

Jim began to gingerly descend the rocky uneven slope.

'Take it easy, kid,' yelled one of the men up above.

But this wasn't the first time Jim had been down Old Smoky; once over the first slippery stage it was comparatively easy going. He reached the bottom and greeted the four men.

He looked at the steer. It was pretty horribly battered but, still quite clear on its flank was the ringed star brand.

'It was shot,' said Able Cornford briefly.

'An' it was a pretty sick cow afore that,' said Hannibal, the eldest of the Lannigan brothers. Hannibal was slow-witted but he was fine with animals and, strangely enough, very quick on the draw when there was any gun-fighting to be done.

Hannibal had always been Jim's favourite brother, that is, next to Clem. But the others – even now they often treated Jim as if he was still a kid. But Hannibal had seen the kid in action in a free-for-all at the Jolly Moses at Jumptown. That was enough for him. Above all he admired guts in any living thing.

'We've bin along to the end o' Smoky an' we've found the trail where the cattle have been driven on into the Gila,' he told Jim.

'So they were rustled!'

' 'Pears so!'

'Wal, have yuh been into the Gila?'

'No, we wuz jist goin' to when a coupla o' the men reported this an' we came back.'

'We'd never ketch up with 'em now,' said brother Kim, in his half-sneering way. The other brother present, taci-

22

turn Jonathon, said nothing as usual.

'Wal, the trail might lead us somewhere anyway,' retorted Jim.

'Oh, we'll go back,' said Abel, the foreman. 'It's pretty plain what happened here. They'd got a sick steer so they drove him to the edge of Old Smoky then shot him. Maybe they figured we wouldn't spot him down here.'

'D'yuh think maybe it's the same people who shot that other steer?' said Kim.

'I'd almost forgotten that,' said Abel. 'I was too concerned about poor ol' Bull bein' shot the same time.'

'Yeh, it was queer about ol' Bull being shot by thet steer,' said Hannibal slowly. 'I wish . . .'

Kim interrupted. 'Maybe he just happened along at the wrong time.'

'Or maybe it *was* robbery after all like your Dad says,' said Abel. 'He blames one o' the M.L.G. bunch. He says all these casual labourers are thieves and cut-throats.'

Jim hardly suppressed a smile. There were some pretty tough customers on Pat Lannigan's own payroll. The old man hired them in the first place supposedly to fight off desert bandits and redskins, but many a 'nester' had been scared off the range by the rough antics of Circle Star hoodlums. They had their cattle shot, their buildings burned and there were one or two mysterious killings that were never laid at anybody's door. It was hardly a laughing matter at that. At times Jim hated his father. The old man had small cause to call other people thieves and cut-throats. It was only because he thought everyone was as ruthless and unscrupulous as himself that made him hate and suspect the M.L.G. people so much.

Jim said 'Bull had a few dollar bills and some nickels in his trouser pocket, that was all. The pouch in the body-belt beneath his gunbelt was empty. It might be that he won a roll playing cards at the Jolly Moses that night. Nobody seems to know. It wasn't a house game, it was a private game an' we can't trace the people Bull played with. I

23

asked around purty fair in the short time I was there an'
drew a blank. I'm goin' back later on to get the sheriff on
the job – if he's returned from his 'business' trip. I did find
out one thing, an' that from some labourers at the M.L.G.
They saw Bull talking outside the Jolly Moses to a middle-
aged man who had either a beard or a bushy moustache.'

Kim laughed sneeringly. 'Jest a cock-an'-bull story I
reckon.'

Abel Cornford interposed hastily. 'Wal, we shan't get no
place standin' around here. I vote we have some chuck an'
then try to make somethin' o' that trail into the Gila.'

CHAPTER FOUR

Pierre Flaubin's Jolly Moses saloon in Jumptown was the Mecca of that particular slice of the Arizona borderlands. Pierre was a Frenchy with a definite dash of Indian blood. He was powerfully built with long black hair and clean-shaven features. Behind his back people called him 'Crow'. He wasn't popular with the riff-raff of the town.

This, however, did not prevent them using his place; there were more girls there, more games, and the best liquor money could buy. Saturday night was their night to howl, often there were free drinks from some good-natured cuss – particularly now the M.L.G. mob had moved in. They had money to burn weekends.

This particular Saturday was no exception as the smoke became thicker, the music louder from the decrepit piano and bull-fiddle; the dancing wilder.

As he moved among the crowds, eyes and ears alert, Jim was pushed and jostled and greeted from all sides. Though he probably didn't realize it, he was the most popular of the Lannigan clan. He had rode into town with a bunch of the boys and gone straight to the sheriff's office only to discover that Walt Eckerton was still out of town. His deputy, Bison Jones, offered his services. But Bison was a dim-wit and Jim didn't avail himself of the offer right then.

Now the boys were drinking and playing cards in a corner while he, with a vague idea in his head of 'maybe pickin' up some information', was browsing around. He

caught sight of Pierre Flaubin standing in the open doorway of his office. He'd been wanting to see Pierre. He
wormed his way through the press and approached him.

The half-breed saloon-owner's grim visage split in a
wide grin.

'Hello, Jeem,' he said. 'Long time no see.'

'Yeh, I bin kinda busy. How've yuh bin, Pierre?'

The other man waved a perfectly manicured brown
hand airily. 'Oh, so-so.' Then his face sobered. 'I heard
about Bull Kinsell. Eet was too bad. I liked Bull.' His face
did not change expression. 'He was a good customer . . .
any clue yet who did it? Ees our good sheriff Walt working
on the case?'

'No clue at all,' said Jim. 'An' sheriff Walt ain't workin'
on it. He's still out of town.'

'Ah, that sheriff,' sighed Pierre with Latin elaboration.
'He ees always out of town. It's a mystery where he goes.
On the spree I theenk.'

'Quite likely. He ain't no great shakes as a sheriff
anyway.'

'No,' said Pierre thoughtfully.

'I thought maybe you could help me as regards Bull,'
continued the younger man.

'How, Jeem?'

'Wal, do you know if Bull won much money here the
night before he was murdered?'

'Eet wasn't a house game yuh know, Jeem.'

'No. I know that.'

'I wasn't here. Cal was. I'll call heem.'

He tried in vain to catch the eye of the barman in question. But Cal was too busy.

'I'll get him,' said Jim, and began to tack perilously
around the floor.

He returned with Cal, a wall-eyed cuss with a scowl.

No, Cal didn't know nothin' about Bull winnin' any
dinero. No, Cal didn't know the guys Bull played with. He
didn't know if they were M.L.G. guys or not. He wouldn't

26

be able to tell 'em again anyway.

Cal went.

With eloquent brows and upturned palms Pierre shrugged to his ears.

'I ought to've fired heem years ago. But . . .' he shrugged again eloquently.

The Jolly Moses was really packed now. For quite a bit Jim had had his eyes on a contingent of M.L.G. men led by Callahan, the big Irishman with hair like dirty hay. They were concentrated at the bar close by where the Circle Star men were playing cards.

Then, as Jim watched, it happened! Big Callahan started forward to the Circle Star table, his men behind him. Jim saw the Irishman's ugly mouth open in a shout but did not hear what he said. He began pressing his way through the crowd. He heard Flaubin shout his name.

He saw Abel Cornford rise and go down again before the huge fists of Callahan. Other Circle Star men were rising. Corny Macintosh, his pard 'Crouch' O'Brien, bronco-buster Mick Lucas, old Charlie Pierce and his pard 'Grubber' Stokes, the Lannigan brothers, Hannibal, towering in action, Kim, dark, vital with his perpetual sneer, dour Ep, and Jonathan, quiet, somewhat of a weakling. Then Jim was with them in a glorious free-for-all.

The Circle Star men were outnumbered by those of the M.L.G., but already many of the townsfolk were siding with the former. Jim could not see Mancy Carter or his *segunda* Pete Listery; the M.L.G. men seemed to be led by the giant Callahan who already had a worthy opponent in Hannibal. Anyway, Jim could not imagine the slick, hard Mancy being mixed up in a brawl like this . . . his mind was brought forcibly back to the present by a rock-like fist bashing him on the side of the head. He went backwards across the table, scattering the cards.

As he rose, through half-closed eyes he saw old Grubber Stokes go down from another blow delivered by the same black-jowled labourer. *He had to get that hombre!*

27

He shook his head vigorously to dispel the fog. Rising, he skirted the table and launched himself at the man. The labourer saw him coming and, with a grin, stepped forward to meet him. Skidding on high-heeled boots Jim threw his body to one side evading the man's swinging right. His own straight left caught the man in the midriff, doubling him up. Jim straightened and bored in. The other man was tough. He straightened too. They met in a flurry of blows. These M.L.G. men all seemed to be built on the same rugged pattern and had obviously learnt their fighting in a tough school.

Jim's lips were crushed against his teeth by another piledriver; searing pain, and the warm salty taste of blood and, as he went down, he cursed himself for not keeping his wits about him. He looked up at his opponent and rolled. The heavy boot just missed his head. Jim grabbed the leg and pulled. The man crashed down beside him.

Jim spat a broken tooth from his mouth as he clutched the top of the table to help himself to his feet. As he looked up in that split second he saw a blue-jeaned man, a grinning man with a black moustache, draw two guns and fire at the two hanging lights. The *hombre* was a crack-shot: one moment garishness, the next pitch darkness.

For a moment the babble of voices was redoubled in volume. Then a terrible scream cut through the sound and the blackness like something alien and uncanny. All sound froze except the breathing of spent and startled men. Then in a corner a woman began to sob with terror.

A familiar voice spoke from the direction of the bar: 'Keep quiet and steell everbody. We're going to light some lamps. I've got a shotgun resting on the bartop and if anybody acts queer I weell start blasting.' Pierre's voice was grim: he meant what he said.

Nobody moved. Nobody wanted to. Everybody had been frozen by that terrible bubbling cry. They welcomed the sparkling light of the hurricane lanterns as the barmen lit them.

The room was filled with light and all heads swivelled hypnotically to the place where the fight had started, where the scream had come from.

The young Circle Star waddy, Corny Macintosh, lay on the boards in a pool of blood with his head hanging grotesquely, almost severed from his body. Abel Cornford was the nearest to the body. His face paled but with a tense expression he went nearer and bent over. When he straightened up he held, with its hilt between his thumb and forefinger, a bloodstained bowie-knife.

The dead man's friend, dark, bitter, hump-shouldered 'Crouch' O'Brien said 'That's Corny's own knife.' His face was expressionless, his eyes gleamed dully.

Most people were stunned by this sudden catastrophe. Free-for-alls were fun, shootings were not unusual. But this sudden callous butchery was unforeseen, almost supernatural.

Pierre Flaubin still stood behind the bar, his hands clenched around the shotgun on the bartop, his dark eyes fixed on the scene.

The shock was wearing off, and most of the watchers' faces now wore their customary hard-bitten expressions. Those at the back began to jostle forward to get a better view.

Jim Lannigan looked around for the grinning ape who had shot out the lights. He saw Callahan standing with a rather puzzled expression on his broad face. But of his sharpshooting colleague there was no sign at all.

Then a voice bawled at the back: 'What's going on here?' The crowd parted and the perspiring moon-face of sheriff Walt Eckerton appeared.

'Ah,' said Jim Lannigan, soberly. 'Just the man we want to see.'

Clem Lannigan and his fiancée, Bessie Crockett, daughter of old Jeb Crockett, livery-man of Jumptown, stood hand in hand. Before them was a newly-built log cabin.

'Wal, that's it, *chiquita*,' said Clem. 'I didn't bring you out here till it was all finished. What d'yuh think of it?'

'It's grand, Clem.' Pretty, blonde, Bessie wasn't a demonstrative girl. The husky tones of her voice and the look in her eyes when she looked up at him told Clem all he wanted to know.

'I've staked out the land too,' he said, swinging her around. 'Look over there – that bluff – that's one corner. An' over there just to the right of the mesquite scrub is another. The other two are beyond the cabin.

'We'll grow our own vegetables. I'm gonna order a few head of beef, an' some hosses. It'll be grand. We'll make out, Bessie. It'll . . .' He was babbling like a love-sick kid, but he stopped dead when he saw the cloud over Bessie's blue eyes.

'What's the matter, *chiquita*?'

'Oh, I was just thinking, Clem. Things 'ud be a lot better if your Dad 'ud see eye to eye with us. An' – an' then there's the things that are happening around here lately. Terrible things. Bull Kinsell, and then that young cowboy in Flaubin's place last night. An' nobody's punished for it. Nobody knows . . . Oh, Clem, how's it all going to end? I – I'm kinda scared, Clem.'

'Yeh, things are kind of uncertain. Nobody knows how it's gonna end. But we mustn't let it interfere with our plans. It can't touch us, Bess.'

'I hope not . . . do you think the M.L.G. people are at the bottom of it like your Dad says?'

'I dunno what to think. I saw Jim this mornin'. He's the only one from home I do see now. He says the M.L.G. people started the ruckus last night, but they had provocation. It seems Corny Macintosh was spoutin' pretty loud about the M.L.G. mob bein' a lot of rustlers and cutthroats an' that big 'Mick' Callahan heard him. That started it . . . nobody figured it'd end like that. An' it's kinda ironic Corny bein' the one to have his throat cut. Walt Eckerton jailed Callahan on suspicion. But he could-

30

n't hold him. Mancy Carter, the M.L.G. ramrod bailed him out this mornin'.'

'Who's Mancy Carter?' said Bessie. 'What's he like?'

'Seems all right tuh me. He's jest a professional ramrod on buildings, an' railways an' such. He certainly keeps them tough Micks in line.'

Clem looked down at Bessie. Her face was still clouded. He gave a rather strained laugh and put his hand around her shoulders, hugging her tight to his side.

'Let's forget it a while,' he said. 'Come on.' They began to walk towards the cabin.

Something passed swiftly over their heads with a buzz like an angry hornet. As the flat echoes of a rifle sounded around them, Jim pushed Bessie to the ground, his arm and half his body shielding her, his other hand drawing his gun.

'Keep down, Bess,' he said. Cautiously he raised his head, looking over to the bluff which formed one corner stone of his homestead. From there he figured the shot had come. There was no movement.

'Clem!' Bessie's anguished cry.

'Keep down,' he shouted harshly, over his shoulder. He was scared. He could never remember being so scared. Getting ready to throw himself flat again at the first sign from that bluff. Awaiting the impact of a slug. But he knew what he was doing. He had to keep his body between Bessie and the man with the rifle. He kept moving on.

Something moved behind the bluff. He had a fleeting glimpse of the crown of a hat. He fired. The hat disappeared. Clem began to run and as he did so heard the beat of hoofs. He reached the crown of the bluff. A horseman was riding away. Already he was out of gunshot range.

He looked back. Bessie was running towards him. He turned his back on the fleeing dry-gulch merchant and ran to meet her. They met and, as he enfolded her in his long arms, she was sobbing with relief.

'I don't think he meant to kill us, Bess,' he said. 'But

31

jest to scare us. For some reason I guess somebody don't want us to settle here.'

'Not your Dad?'

Clem grinned. 'Gosh, no. Dad don't fight thataway.' But despite his easy assurance there was a little seed of doubt already planted in his mind.

Bessie's nervousness and tears had changed to rage. Her eyes blazed as she stood away from Clem and said 'Well, whoever they are we won't let 'em scare us. We'll carry on. We'll get married next week just like we planned.'

CHAPTER FIVE

Abel Cornford's face was grave. He held the wad of bills in his hand as if they were malignant life. Jim folded the bedroll up again and pushed it under the bunk. The two men were alone in the Circle Star bunkhouse.

'Wal,' said Abel. 'I guess that ties it up. There don't seem much doubt that Corny Macintosh bushwhacked Bull Kinsell and robbed him o' his roll. Where else would he get such a pile of money? I know for a fact that he lost his own gamblin' at the Jolly Moses last week.'

'Mebbe Crouch O'Brien 'ud tell us more about it,' offered Jim.

'Yeh, mebbe. I'll see if I can get him in here.' Abel went to the door and opened it.

A rider was going past the corral. 'Benny,' shouted Abel. The man turned his head, stopped his horse. 'Ridin' down by the Nawth line-hut, Benny?' asked Abel.

'Yep.'

'Find Crouch O'Brien then, will yuh, an' send him here. Tell him I want him urgent.'

'All right, Abel. I'll do that.' The man urged his horse forward. He went off at a gallop.

Abel re-entered the bunkhouse and sat on a chair by the table. 'I'll get some coffee,' said Jim and he left.

He had returned and they had almost finished their drinks when Crouch O'Brien entered the bunkhouse.

'Quick work, Crouch,' said Abel.

The dark, queer shouldered man did not smile. His

33

face wore its usual lowering look. He was a good man about the ranch, but always taciturn and morose as if he thought his twisted shoulders, one higher than the other and humped, made him different to the other men. Maybe they had done wrong to dub him 'Crouch' when he first rode in with Corny Macintosh, twelve months ago – but it was too late now. Crouch he was, and Crouch he remained until his queer tale was ended.

He said 'What's bitin' yuh, Abel?'

The foreman put the wad of money on the table.

'We found this in Corny's bedroll,' he said. 'Got any idea how he came by it?'

For a moment something like a smile appeared on the other's dark face. Then it vanished as he said 'Corny never had that much money.'

'Ain't it right that Corny lost his last pay entirely at the Jolly Moses?'

'Yeh.'

'Then how come this was in his bedroll?'

'I dunno. We wuz pards. I allus knew what he'd got. He useter borrow money off me. He borrowed three dollars a coupla days ago.'

'This was in his bedroll,' insisted Abel. 'How did it get there? How did Corny get it?'

Crouch O'Brien's eyes smouldered. 'I know what yuh think,' he said. 'You think Corny shot Bull Kinsell an' stole that roll off'n him. Corny wouldn't do that. I know him. But I'll tell yuh somethin' else . . .'

'What's that?'

'Corny shot that steer. It went lame an' he shot it. Then he forgot to report. Then when he heard Bull had been shot at the same place he wuz too scared to report. He figured if he did folks'd think he'd killed Bull as well.'

'Maybe he did. He'd got the money. We figured you might be able to tell us somethin' about that.'

Crouch's face remained expressionless, but his misshapen body seemed to tense.

34

'Look,' he said. 'Even if Corny did do it, I know nothin'
about it. I wasn't married to him. An' I tell yuh he didn't.
I know Corny better'n any of yuh. The only thing I can say
is I guess the money was planted there.'

'Maybe it was,' said Abel softly. 'All right, Crouch. But
yuh must understand we shall hafta hand this money over
to the sheriff an' tell him where we found it.'

'Do what you like with it!' snarled Crouch as he turned
on his heels.

The door banged behind him.

That afternoon Jim and Abel rode out into the Gila
Desert. They followed a faintly discernible cattle-trail, a
trail already being obliterated by shifting sand. At times it
vanished and they had to cast around until they picked up
the other broken end. All around them was arid waste
dotted with stunted plants and shrubs, and outcrops of
rock like ugly warts on the landscape. The sun was half
blinding as they rode into its glare, now and then gusts of
hot wind blew the fine biting sand into their faces, sticking
there, caking in the heat on their eyes and lips.

When they were about a mile and a half past Old Smoky
Gulch Abel said:

'I figure we'll be coming to the rocks soon. That's as far
as we could follow it. After that we couldn't find a trace.
We fished around a bit, then darkness fell an' we had to
light out for home. None of us fancied a night out here.'

'Nor would I,' said Jim.

A few minutes later they halted where the sand ended
and the ground was hard and flinty.

'The end o' the trail,' said Abel. 'From here they might
have gone in any direction. You could drive a million head
across this stuff without leavin' a trail.'

'Shore could,' said Jim. 'Still, we may as well cast
around a bit, we may pick somethin' up.'

They separated and rode slowly in half-circles, their
heads bent, their eyes searching the ground.

Jim's eyes began to water as the sun-glare hit the hard crystally ground, and batted back into his face. He pulled his hat-brim as low as possible.

Then suddenly he saw something on the rock almost beneath his horse's feet. Something still and black, he thought at first it was a dead and shrivelled snake. He dismounted and bent closer. Then he realized it was just a length of coiled leather, part of a whip or something. He picked it up. It wasn't a whip but the leather hat-band from a sombrero, the sort that are just looped around and knotted. It had come loose from somebody's hat and fallen to the ground unnoticed.

Jim was dubious about it being any sort of a clue. He looked at it more closely and his eyes brightened with interest. A maker's name was stamped in tiny letters on its under side. Jim spelled out 'Portwin's, Kansas City'. His interest awakened. The hat-band looked fairly new, too, still a glossy black, unmarked by dirt or sweat-marks. Maybe one of the storekeepers in Jumptown would know something about it.

Jim tucked it into the capacious pocket of his chaps, and remounting his horse, cantered after Abel.

He showed the hat-band to the foreman and they speculated awhile. Then they made tracks for Jumptown. They had to see sheriff Eckerton anyway.

Dusk was falling when they entered the cowtown.

'I vote we eat afore we do any more amateur detective work,' said Jim. He was a healthy young animal and right now he certainly needed some fodder.

'I'm suttinly in favour with what you jest said, young Jim,' said Abel.

He led the way instinctively to the Jolly Moses. They took their horses to the small stables beside the saloon and left them in the charge of the half-witted youth there known as 'Puffing Billy', because although eighteen years of age he still liked to play trains and often did 'chuff chuffing' up and down the main street with his elbows

36

going like pistons. A queer fact was that he'd been involved in a train accident when he was a kid. Both his young parents had been killed.

It was early yet and the Jolly Moses was quiet. There was nobody at all at the bar, but a few tables were occupied with diners who had their likker beside their plates.

The wall-eyed Cal bustled in from the back place, scowled at the new arrivals and bawled 'Steak, chips, *frijoles*!'

Jim and Abel both nodded. 'All right,' Abel yelled back. 'Make that two – an' long beers.'

Still scowling but sharp as a tack Cal returned almost immediately with the meals. Then he drew them two long beers. Both men took appreciative swigs.

'I certainly needed that,' said Abel reaching for his knife and fork.

Jim followed his example. He said 'Say, if we split up afterwards, you go tuh see the sheriff an' I'll see about this hat-band.'

'Cain't hardly wait to get your nose tuh the scent again, can yuh?' said Abel.

Jim grinned. Then he became serious. 'We gotta get tuh the bottom of all this ain't we?'

'We suttinly have. An' we'll do jest what yuh say.'

Jim went first to Jumptown's one and only tailor, Mortimer Cuzzons, who kept the dusty little shop right next to the bank.

Mortimer turned up his Grecian nose at the hat-band.

'That's common fancy stuff,' he said. 'I don't have stuff like that in my shop. Those things are turned out in millions and sold in stores all over the country. Pop Cantell has probably got a stock in right now.'

Pop Cantell kept the general stores a few doors away from the tailors. He was a frail, gentle, white-haired old *hombre*, everybody was very welcome in his all-purpose stores.

He greeted Jim gently, his faded eyes twinkling behind

his spectacles. Jim showed him the hat-band. Pop smiled and pointed to a dim corner of the stores.

'There's a pile of 'em over there, Jim,' he said. 'Help y'self.'

The young man was a mite taken aback. However, he strolled with studied nonchalance over to the corner and began to grub around. A customer entered the shop and he pretended to be studying a hat very closely. When the customer had gone he took the hat across to Pop.

'There's all sorts o' fancy stuff there, ain't there,' he said. 'But, I reckon this is the sort of hat that band came off. What d'you think, Pop.'

'I reckon you're right, Jim,' he said.

'It says on this hatband that it comes from 'Portwins, Kansas City.' Do all your hats come from Kansas City, Pop?'

'I get that particular line from Kansas City. The others come from different places.'

'That's somethin' anyway.' said Jim.

Pop didn't ask him: why all the questions? He knew young Jim Lannigan wouldn't come a-pestering him unless there was some good reason behind it.

'I suppose these hats can be got in stores all over the States?'

'I dessay,' said Pop. 'They seem purty popular.'

Jim looked at the high chocolate-coloured curly-brimmed monstrosity critically. Well, there was no accounting for tastes.

'Sold many o' these partic'ler kind lately?' he asked.

'Wal, that's hard tuh say, Jim,' said Pop. 'I sell purty well from time to time. An' there's so many different kinds. I dessay I've sold about half a dozen of that kind within the last week besides some o' the other kinds as well. There's quite a lot of strangers in town lately.'

'Have you sold one lately to anybody you know?'

'I can't remember – except young 'Puffin' Billy' over the stables. He bought one the other day.'

'Can you describe anybody who's bought one lately?'

'Wal, if I remember rightly the last one o' that kind I sold a coupla days ago to a big feller with a big black moustache.'

Jim looked more interested. 'Wore overalls, did he?'

'Yeh, now you come to mention it, I think he did.'

'Mebbe he was one o' the people who are helpin' tuh build that new ranch then?'

'Yeh, I thought that . . . still, I dessay most of the strangers who come in come from there.'

'Can yuh think of anybody else who bought a hat?'

'Wal; there was one queer tall *hombre* with red hair. I cain't remembered whether he had one o' them sort or one o' the others though.'

'Hum,' said Jim. 'Wal, thanks anyway, Pop. Give me some .44 shells will yuh?'

He made his purchase, returned the monstrous sombrero to its pile and, with another 'thanks', and an *adios* to Pop, left the stores.

He was thoughtful. A black-moustached or black-bearded man had been seen talking to Bull Kinsell that night here; a black moustached man had shot out the lights at the Jolly Moses just before Corny Macintosh was murdered. Maybe it was just a coincidence. There were hundreds of big black moustaches about. He'd got 'em on the brain. And to return to the M.L.G. He kept returning to the M.L.G. Anyway, it was M.L.G. men who first told him about the black moustached man in the first place, so that kind of complicated things. Maybe he was getting so he wanted to lay the whole villainous caboodle at the M.L.G. doors. Maybe he was like his Dad – getting prejudiced against the M.L.G.

He met Abel. Abel said 'Wal, I've seen Walt Eckerton. He says there ain't no conclusive proof against Corny Macintosh . . .'

'We know that. We don't want to blacken a dead man's name. We'd sooner clear it.'

'Yeh,' said Abel.

39

'Maybe the money was planted in Corny's bedroll like Crouch O'Brien said.'

'I told the sheriff all that,' said Abel, with monumental patience. 'He says he'll start investigating – he'll make enquiries.'

'Did yuh tell him I'd done most o' that while he was highfalutin' round the countryside?'

'I didn't want to offend him.'

'Did yuh leave the money with him?'

'Yeh.'

Jim grinned. 'Next thing yuh know he'll be goin' on the spree with that.'

'If he don't do nothing within a few days I'm gonna ask him for it back. Corny might have some next o' kin . . .'

'Yeh,' said Jim. 'I hope Eckerton can clear it up. I didn't like Corny overmuch, but I shouldn't like to think he murdered Bull. If he didn't I'd like to get my hands on the *hombre* who did.'

They were leaving Jumptown now and taking the trail for home. Jim told Abel of his interview with Pop Cantell.

CHAPTER SIX

Bessie Crockett and Clem Lannigan got married in the little frame chapel at the top of the main street of Jumptown. The preacher officiating was the Reverend Maxwell Dobrez, tall, dark, saturine, with his mournful sing-song voice. Grizzled, cheery old Jeb Crockett, keeper of the livery stable, gave the bride away. Jim Lannigan was best man.

Stout, motherly Mrs Crockett was there cheering everyone up. It was plain to see where Bessie got her effervescent good spirits. Her widowed Aunt Mab, proprietor of Jumptown's only milliners was there too. And quite a sizeable bunch of townsfolk, friends of the Crocketts, plus the usual lounging sightseers. But Jim was the only member of the Lannigan clan who was present.

Jim was disappointed. He knew Abel Cornford would have liked to come, but was too busy at the ranch. But he had expected his brother, Hannibal. There was no doubt that although he was tough, Jim's big simple elder brother was still very much under the domination of his father. And the other three, Kim, Ep, Jonathon, were just plain scared.

Half-a-dozen buggies stood outside the chapel and after the ceremony the happy couple, Mr and Mrs Crockett and all the older guests piled in these. The younger people, Jim amongst them, came along on horseback, whooping the party along as they made for Clem's little cabin on the range.

There the wedding spread was already laid. The cabin, a cosy two-roomed affair, was soon packed with merry well-wishers. Standing almost unnoticed just inside the door-way, Jim wondered if Clem was as disappointed as he was at not seeing any more of the family there. He was probably too happy to care. With his smiling bride beside him he certainly looked it. Jim looked about him. A cosy little place. For a few moments he had feelings foreign to his nature. He had always planned to leave home some day – maybe after this mysterious business was cleared up – and seek pastures new. But maybe if he met a girl like Bessie he'd want to homestead right here. The range was good and he guessed one place was as good as another really. Funny what a woman could do to a man. He hadn't had the experience himself yet, so he didn't really know what he'd do in the circumstances. But this was still a mighty cosy little crib.

Night enveloped the range and the little cabin in the hollow a mile from the edge of Old Smoky where the undefined trail ran into the Gila.

Further out a sizeable herd of Circle Star cattle were bedded-down, the bovine mass shifting now and then with the skittering of dogies. On the left flank Vic Porter rode slowly, singing plaintively an obscene bar-room ditty. Vic was a tough kid, a gunfighter who had killed two men over the border in a Texas town. He was on the run, and, asking no questions, Pat Lannigan had taken him in. Fighting rannies like Vic usually came in useful.

Vic's two partners on the left flank were 'Gunner' Malone, ex-prizefighter and his whining pard, 'Creepy' Duprez, a little half-breed who seemed to enjoy the 'Gunner's' constant bullying. Gunner tried to bully anybody who came along, so seeing the big ape was the same shift with him, Vic had wisely kept away from him. He didn't want to have to put a slug in Gunner's pot-belly. However, he sang out to the big ape and his little man

42

from time to time.

Over on the right flank were Jimmy Eplethwaite, 'One-eye' Gibson and Rollo Penneli. In the van were 'Crouch' O'Brien and, in place of Crouch's pard, the late lamented Corny, a hard-bitten young new hand called Squint O'Brien. It amused old Pat's sardonic humour to have two O'Brien's together. And two such widely-different types: 'Crouch', morose and taciturn, Squint a braggart with a chip on his shoulder.

It was Vic Porter who heard the hoofbeats first. He shouted to Gunner and Creepy. The wind carried his voice away. He received no answer, and figured they hadn't heard him. He shouted again and thought he heard an answering cry, but by then he could see the bunch of galloping horsemen, their faces black, the glint of steel in the hands.

Vic didn't lack guts but he knew he didn't stand a chance if he stayed there. He galloped his horse along the fringe of the herd towards Gunner and Creepy. His gun was out. He fired twice at the oncoming horsemen. To his nervous imagination there seemed to be hundreds of them. He had the satisfaction of seeing a horse crash to the ground, its rider pitching over its head and falling in front of it.

Then the raiders began to fire back. Vic slid Indian-fashion against his horse's flank, shielded by the beast's body, triggering across his back. Miraculously they were not hit.

The cattle began to shift and low, and the main body of the attackers carried on while about half-a-dozen broke away and made for Vic. As he saw them coming, out of his other eye he saw the ape-like figure of Gunner Malone hunched on his rawboned nag before him. And beside Gunner the smaller bunched figure on the smaller horse, of Creepy Duprez. Then the ill-assorted pair saw the half-dozen riders bearing down on them and turned to flee.

'You yeller-livered bastards,' screamed Vic. Odds being

now only two to one he had figured they stood a chance. He straightened up, swerving his horse's head, making after Gunner and Creepy, and half-turning in the saddle, firing back at the raiders.

He 'yipped' crazily as he saw one rider catapulted from his mount. Then a red-hot leaden fist smote him in the side, and he was thrust from his mount, rolling in folds of blackness.

The horsemen swept past him, one flailing hoof narrowly missing his head. He lay with his face in cool grass, his inside burning. Slowly, agonizingly, he raised his head. Then he grinned with ironic glee as he saw Gunner and Creepy go down before their pursuers' fire. If the bastards hadn't ran away . . . nausea overcame him and his head dropped again. The returning horsemen swept past without a glance at his prone body. Their eyes glinted through the slits in the black kerchiefs they wore covering their faces.

There was more shooting: the gang had met up with the three night-riders on the other flank. Eplethwaite, Gibson and Pennelli had a better chance. The firing had warned them. But they didn't know what they were up against until the gang swept round the front of the herd. Then it was too late. Eplethwaite and Penneli went down. 'One-eye' Gibson turned his horse's head and made a bolt for it. He galloped for the back of the herd yelling a warning to the two O'Briens. They came to meet him then, seeing the oncoming raiders, outnumbering them by so many, turned to run with him. In the ranks of the attackers somebody barked an order and half-a-dozen men broke away to chase the fugitives. The rest turned back.

If they didn't act fast they would have a man-sized stampede on their hands. More orders were barked. The men split, spread out. The herd began to move. The black-masked raiders, men who obviously knew their job, whoever they were, began to haze the leaders in one direction. Towards the Gila Desert.

44

Clem Lannigan heard the thunder of the approaching mass and rising quietly from beside his bride began to dress in silent haste. It sounded like some dumb cowboy had started a stampede. Maybe he wouldn't be able to do anything on his own, but he'd go out and see what was going on. He'd be able to give directions to anybody who was after them. By the sound of things it was quite proba-ble they were heading straight for the lip of Old Smoky. Clem's mind was racing: he shuddered at the thought of the loss to his father if the cattle did plunge into the gulch, while at the same time, figuring it might teach the old man a lesson anyway. The arrival of the M.L.G. had cracked his complacence a little, a thing like this would maybe crack it still more, make him realize that things could happen to him just like they had happened to dozens of little men he had hounded from the range.

As he closed the cabin door behind him he did not know that Bessie had sat up in bed, hearing the running cattle too. He did not hear her whispered 'Clem'.

He saddled his horse in the little leanto and rode out. It was a dark, moonless night, the stars very high and a fitful breeze soughing from time to time. The sound of cattle was much nearer now. Clem paused to intercept its direction, then, turning his horse's head slightly, began to ride. He did not see Bessie close the cabin door behind her and run to the small stable to get her own mount.

There were lots of things Clem did not know or under-stand – or even stop to think about. He rode recklessly forward hoping only to be able to help the father who had so lately turned him down.

He saw the shifting, now almost mechanical, mass moving swiftly, but not wild now, he saw the riders with them and was relieved. They'd caught up with 'em anyway. Hot dog! Might as well ride forward and say hello. He galloped nearer.

The herd had gone. The range was quiet again. As quiet as death with the wind moaning a dirge. Slowly, painfully, Vic Porter rose to his knees. He looked around. Just darkness. He got to his feet, stumbled a few paces, then went down again. The grass was damp beneath his hands. He buried his forehead in its coolness and gasped with pain. The hole in his side felt as big as a bucket. He began to crawl forward.

As long as he could keep up on his hands and knees like this and keep moving he'd get on. He felt as if he had gone miles when he saw the bodies of Gunner and Creepy. Then he knew he hadn't gone very many yards. He didn't stop to see whether his erstwhile night-pardners were dead. They looked that way.

He could not bend his one leg because of the terrible pain it caused in his side. He dragged it, working the other one and his hands and elbows mechanically. He tried to keep his head and shoulders up. He knew that if he let them drop he'd be down again and finished. With chances of being attacked by coyotes or prairie dogs or dying out here from loss of blood.

There was no knowing whether any of the rustlers were still moseying around. Rot their stinking hides! He began to curse with hoarse and painful fluency as he crawled along. It was small relief!

Only his arms and his one leg moved – and his lips. His mind was dead. He was wriggling along in a dream and did not see the horseman until the horse's legs were almost touching him, and the horseman spoke. Then the rider was down beside him and lifting him with strong arms. Before he fainted Vic Porter realized his deliverer was Hannibal Lannigan. There was something very comforting about Hannnibal.

The big Lannigan brother had not been able to sleep. Strangely for such a stolid character, he had periodical attacks of what he called 'the jumps'. He had got the 'jumps' tonight, so went and saddled his horse. He thought maybe he'd go out and say 'hello' to the night-riders. The nearest were about three miles out – a mere canter. He was about two miles from the ranch-house when he thought he heard shots. Maybe the wind was playing him tricks – however he spurred his horse to a gallop.

Vic Porter was pretty far gone when he picked him up and turned for home.

CHAPTER SEVEN

Old Pat Lannigan himself led the boys out that night, leaving only a skeleton staff to guard the ranch buildings. They met Crouch O'Brien walking back home with his saddle under his arm. He was unhurt but his horse had been shot. They picked up four riderless horses, but didn't find Crouch's until later. It has been shot all right – right through the back of the head. It must have been a near escape for the misshapen little ranny. They found the rest of the night-riders, too. Six of them. All dead.

Old Pat's language was vitriolic. Most of the others were too coldly savage to speak. The trail of the rustled cattle was pretty plain to see – there had been a sizeable herd. They were following this when, coming over the rise to take the down-grade where the plain sloped to Old Smoky, they saw the fire.

With an oath, young Jim Lannigan said 'That's Clem's homestead.'

By the time they got down there the place was just a heap of fallen logs, which the flames were hungrily devouring. One thought was in the minds of all those present, but until the flames had subsided they could not prove or disprove their horrible suspicions.

Finally old Pat said 'Abel, you carry on with the men an' follow the trail. You may be able to catch up wi' the buzzards. Me and the five boys'll stay here.'

So Abel Cornford led the men on while the old man and his five sons, sick at heart, waited by the flaming ruins.

Jim and Hannibal rode slowly, in ever-widening circles, round and round the conflagration, looking vainly for something – anything – that might help them to make up their minds one way or another! They didn't find a thing.

When hopelessly they finally returned to the others the fire had almost burnt itself out. The five brothers dismounted and, watched by their father, like a misshapen statue on his rawboned mare, began to kick about in the remains with their riding boots.

When they returned and told him they had found nothing, he did not speak for a moment.

Finally he said ' 'Pears like they got away then.'

'Yeh, but where did they go?' said Kim.

'Maybe the rustlers kidnapped 'em,' said Hannibal, bluntly.

'Whatever happened we shan't get tuh know about it by just gabbing hyar,' said Pat harshly. He turned his horse. 'C'mon, we'll follow the trail after the others.'

They caught up with them in the Gila Desert, motionless in a group where the sand gave way to rock and the trail disappeared.

Old Pat released another stream of invective, concluding with saying 'I'm figuring we oughta look for the instigators of all this much closer home.'

Beside him young Jim reflected the old man was still harping on the M.L.G. Maybe he was right at that! Pat was shaking with rage. There was no knowing what he might do, but Jim had a pretty good guess.

'C'mon,' said the old man, harshly. 'We shan't find nothin' hyar till daylight.'

The others followed him like sheep as he turned back on the trail. They skirted Old Smoky at a gallop. Jim's guess had been right. Old Pat was leading them to the M.L.G.

However, when they got in the vicinity of the new buildings, Pat's wrath had subsided a little, he was not riding so fast.

When a guard challenged them he shouted harshly 'I

should keep your finger off that trigger if I were you, pardner. We've only come tuh do a little investigatin'. But
there's quite a sizeable passel of us.'

The guard wisely let them by. Pat halted them in the
clearing opposite Mancy Carter's cabin.

There was no activity, the camp was in darkness. But
now things began to stir, lanterns were lit, men began to
form a glowering circle around the disturbers of the
peace. Even half-dressed they looked a tough bunch. No
tougher than the Circle Star men, however, who, though
their leaders had led them into a ticklish spot, were not a
bit concerned.

'Wal, if our rustlers came from here they certainly got
back into their holes purty quick,' said Jim.

There was a stir in the ever increasing, encircling ranks.
They broke and, escorted by two stalwards with lanterns,
Pete Listery, Carter's little *segunda*, came forward. He was
clad only in shirt, trousers, and high boots. He looked a
nondescript little figure, a little rat with tousled colourless
hair and blinking eyes.

He looked up at the silently grouped horsemen and
opened his mouth to speak. Then old Pat boomed
'Where's Mancy Carter?'

Whatever Listery meant to say he forgot it in favour of
answering the old man's question – in a bewildered tone
of voice: 'He ain't here. He very seldom stays here o'
nights. He mostly sleeps in town.'

'What time did he go out tonight?'

'Oh, purty early I guess. About 9.30.'

'Did anybody go with him?'

'Naw, I don't think so. Some o' the boys went, too. But
they went after.'

'How many o' the boys?'

'Oh, 'bout a coupla dozen.'

'Have they come back?'

'No. They'll stay there all night an' come back in the
morning like they allus do.'

'Anybody else bin out o' the camp since then?'

'No, not as I know about.'

'An' you ain't heard nothin'?'

Listery looked puzzled. 'N . . . no.' He turned to his men as if for confirmation. They growled, rather ominously it seemed.

Their attitude seemed to give the little man courage. He drew himself up. 'Why all the questions?' he said.

'My cattle have been rustled. My son's cabin has been burnt to the ground. My son and his wife have disappeared.' Pat's voice got harsher as each fact fed his rage.

But Listery now had the bit between his teeth. 'How should that concern us?' he said. 'Why should you wake us up in the middle of the night to tell us all this?'

Pat's mercurial rage subsided again. Listery seemed genuinely indignant. The old man lied. 'We thought maybe the rustlers drove the cattle this way. We thought maybe' you'd heard somethin'.' He knew he was beat. He knew he had no proof to back up his suspicions, no right to wake up the sleeping (?) camp in this way.

'Nobody's heard nothin'.' said Listery, sullenly.

'Wal, in that case, I guess we'll hafter mosey along,' said Pat. He turned his horse. His men followed suit. The encircling mob watched sullenly. Nobody spoke until Pat turned in his saddle and shouted, 'Be sure to tell Carter we called, won't you?'

The following morning old Pat and his *segunda*, Abel Cornford, rode into Jumptown to see sheriff Walt Eckerton, and also to see if maybe Clem and Bessie had taken shelter there. The sheriff was in for a stormy interview no doubt.

Jim, Hannibal, Kim, Ep and Jonathon, together with 'Crouch' O'Brien, Mick Lucas, the wrangler, and two other tough rannies called 'Jingo' Embers and 'Kansas' Brown, rode once again into the Gila on the trail of the rustlers. Or at least on the trail of the stolen cattle – old Pat still insisted the rustlers were much closer, if not at the

51

M.L.G. in Jumptown. Nobody had much hopes of the old man and his foreman finding Clem and his wife in Jumptown. The general opinion was that the rustlers had taken the pair with them. Old Pat was very rich – maybe a ransom would be asked for. The brothers were anxious. Even their hardbitten parents were worried, although they had had more practice at concealing their emotions. Until now they had become emotionless, ruthless, egotistical. But now they were beginning to realize they were not as all-powerful as they thought. Little wonder they laid all the blame on the newly-arrived M.L.G., more far-reaching, more powerful than they could ever be. For years they had dominated Old Smoky range, keeping their territory by ruthless means. They suspected the M.L.G. of using the same means to deprive them of what was theirs by right of conquest. They sought no compromise. Maybe they were right . . . *maybe.*

The five brothers and their four companions halted in the old place where the trail ended on the hard rock surface. 'Jingo' Embers, middle-aged, dark, cruel-looking, dismounted from his horse. He had been raised in Indian country, a rare white friend to Apaches who had taught him their lore and arts. He had rode into the Circle Star about eighteen months ago and demanded a job. Old Pat liked his independent, impertinent manner and set him on. He soon proved his worth – at cowpunching and fighting. He was not popular with the rest of the men. The chip on his shoulder was sizeable and up till now nobody had succeeded in knocking it off. Many said he was half-Indian. Whether or not he certainly was a great tracker.

The other men sat on their horses and watched him as, body crouched, he moved slowly forward like a hound on the scent, oblivious of everything else. Suddenly he looked up and beckoned the others forward.

He mounted his horse and led them across the rocky waste, his practised eyes studying the ground, noting prints that were invisible to the others. From time to time he halted them while he dismounted and ranged back and forth until once more he was sure, and they pressed on again.

The territory they covered now was some prehistoric geological freak, the sort of landscape only to be found in Arizona, rocky, or at the best, covered with loose shale. Strange outcrops of flinty bounders, stunted cacti and hybrid desert scrub. The only living things lizards, like little monsters, and wheeling buzzards, who doubtless had seen other travellers who had come to grief in this desolate hellspot and were hoping in their tiny brains that the same fate would befall these nine horsemen. Then what glorious pickings there would be!

Jingo bent and picked something up. He handed it to Hannibal Lannigan. It was the heel from a high-heeled riding-boot.

Hannibal made no comment. He nodded briefly and put the heel in his chap's pocket.

Pat Lannigan banged a huge fist down on the sheriff's desk and, wedged behind it, Walt Eckerton's bulk trembled like a jelly with the vibrations from the blow.

'I tell yuh, Walt, somethin's gotta be done. You ain't gonna wriggle out o' this. If you try to I'll raise such a stink to blow you an' your damned office across the Rio. My son an' his wife 'uv disappeared. They ain't in town. I figured they might be hiding 'em at the M.L.G. camp . . .'

'But Pat . . .'

'You find 'em,' bawled Pat. 'Or I'll take this country apart. Form posses – get after 'em – get after the stolen cattle. That's what you're paid for.'

'I'll do muh best, Pat. I'll . . .' the rest of the sheriff's speech was cut off by the door banging behind the old man and Abel Cornford. He blew out a gusty breath of relief.

He rose and going to the window watched them cross the street. Then he turned back to his desk and began to buckle on his gunbelt.

As Pat and Abel crossed the street two men came out of the bank almost opposite the sheriff's office. The big one in the forefront was Mancy Carter. Behind him trailed Pete Listery. Carter saw the two Circle Star men and changing his direction made for them. Rather reluctantly it seemed, Listery followed him.

Abel Cornford nudged old Pat. 'Look who's here,' he said.

Carter halted before them. He looked directly at Pat. He said: 'My foreman tells me you caused quite a ruckus at our camp last night.' It was a bold statement of fact spoken in a level unemotional voice.

Pat looked at him and grunted.

Carter said: 'Listery also says you made certain insinuations. Can you prove 'em?'

'No,' said Pat, flatly. 'Mebbe I aim to.'

'You're at liberty to try,' Carter told him. 'But right now I'm warning you. Don't come bawling down to the M.L.G. like a mad bull every time somethin' happens on your own ground. From now on I'm giving all my men orders to shoot trespassers on sight.'

'Why, yuh mealy-mouthed skunk!' Pat's hand flashed to his gun. Just in time Abel Cornford caught his wrist. Carter hooked one thumb in his belt very close to his own gun. 'If you were a mite younger . . .'

'Lemme go, Abel, darn yuh!' said Pat.

He broke away and swung at Carter. The M.L.G. man side-stepped neatly. When Pat turned he was still there, a half-smile on his thin lips beneath the pencilled moustache. Pat charged again – right into the soft bulk of sheriff Walt Eckerton, who had just arrived. There was a titter from the rapidly-growing ranks of the watching loungers as the sheriff emitted a loud, painful grunt.

Abel caught hold of Pat once more.

'Now, Pat,' said the sheriff, wheezily. 'No brawlin' on the main street, please.' He turned to Carter. 'Git goin'.'

Pat had broken away from Abel and the sheriff, and,

54

perversely, did not follow the two M.L.G. men. Instead he turned on the facetious watchers.

'What's the matter with you grinning apes?' he yelled.

Abel wasn't near enough to stop him this time. His gun was out, and he had the lot of them covered.

'Dance, you bastards!' he said, and threw down on them, his Colt booming, spitting flame and lead.

Slugs tore up the sidewalk at the loungers' feet. They jumped, shuffled, then as one man, turned and fled.

Abel Cornford grinned shakily. Walt Eckerton mopped his streaming brow. 'Godamighty!' he said.

CHAPTER EIGHT

It was a definite trail, the rock surface polished smooth and almost white by the passage of thousands of cattle over a period of many years.

'I might've figured that,' said Jingo Embers.

'I never knew there was a trail across the Gila,' said Jim Lannigan.

'Yeh,' said Jingo. 'It's a very old one. The Injuns used to use it.'

'Must've been a mighty heap o' cattle to make a mark on this stuff,' said Hannibal. 'C'mon, let's follow it.'

'But which way?' said Jingo patiently. 'Which way did they go?'

Hannibal blinked. 'Don't yuh know?'

'I ain't a miracle-man,' said Jingo. 'But I'll try and find out.' He dismounted from his horse.

Ten minutes later he said: 'I think mebbe this way. But don't blame me if I'm wrong.'

He remounted and led the way.

Just before noon they hit the sand again. Here the desert was not so harsh as the Smoky range country. There was more vegetation, patches of grass and trees, and cattle-trails that crossed and re-crossed in a maddening jig-saw. Jingo confessed himself beaten.

'Wal, we might as well carry on till we hit the range again,' said Hannibal. 'I ain't hankering to go back through that desert.'

Everyone agreed upon this. 'We might find a place to

eat an' rest up,' said Jim. 'An' a straight trail back home.'

They chose a beaten cattle track, one of the many, that they figured would lead them out of the desert again. They followed this for so long that most of them thought they had made an error and were forging inwards instead of out. But Jingo, with that extra sense of his, said he reckoned they were on the right track all right – it just seemed a long while, that's all.

However, there were relieved ejaculations when they did finally sight grassland and were definitely sure it was not just a trick of the terrific mid-day sun.

'Oh, for a quart of nice cool root beer,' said Jim Lannigan.

The rest of them echoed his sentiments, adding their own particular favourites. For a moment the object of their long ride was forgotten. Little did they know how soon it would be before they had a terrible reminder of it.

They followed now a clear trail into the range, grassland as lush as that by Old Smoky. A signboard beside the trail attracted their attention. They stopped to read it. It said

THIS RANGE BELONGS TO THE
WAGON WHEEL RANCH
TRAMPS AND NESTERS – KEEP OUT

'Somebody has the same idea as the old man,' said Kim Lannigan sardonically.

A few moments later two riders crossed the trail in front of them. They stared at the strangers, but did not halt. A little later, over to the right of them, the little band saw a sizeable bunch of cattle. Then a rocky bluff obscured the view. They were passing directly alongside this at a distance of about a hundred and fifty yards, when a rifle shot echoed and a spurt of dust was kicked up just in front of Hannibal's horse. The sniper had misjudged his range.

The shot scared Hannibal's horse and he bounded

forward. The others followed almost instinctively. Kim was a decent way behind. The sniper's head rose above his cover as he sighted his rifle to take a snapshot at the fleeing men. Kim's rifle was already out of its scabbard. Kim elevated it and fired. With a gutteral cry of surprise and agony the bushwhacker rolled from his perch.

In a moment the little bunch were around the body. Kim dismounted and turned it callously over with his foot. It was now the very dead remains of a flamboyantly-dressed Mexican. Kim's slug had got him right through the side of the head.

'Nice shootin',' said Hannibal.

'But why was he shootin' at us, that's what I'd like to know,' said brother Jonathon.

'Probably a guard o' some kind,' said brother Ep.

Young brother Jim had something very different to say. 'Look out! We've got company!'

Eight heads swivelled in the same direction as Jim's, eyeing the band of horsemen, a dozen or more, sweeping down on them.

Kim remounted. Jim and Hannibal who had ridden side by side all through the journey, were now a little way to the front.

'Take your hands away from your guns,' said Hannibal. 'Wait for a move from them.' It was at times like these his brain worked its sharpest. He was on his mettle.

The riders came nearer, led by a tall, wide-shouldered man on a big black stallion. This man reined in directly opposite Hannibal and Jim. The others grouped behind him. They were a hard-looking bunch, but no harder than the travel-stained nine who confronted them.

The big man was very brown and handsome and yellow hair flowed from under his black sombrero. He reminded Jim Lannigan of somebody, but the younker couldn't set his mind on who right then.

The big man indicated the dead Mexican with an unemotional jerk of his thumb.

'Who did this?' he asked tonelessly.

'I did,' said Kim, with his sneering half-grin. 'He fired on us first,' said Hannibal.

'He had orders to fire on any trespassers!' said the big feller, his lips drawn back in a half-snarl, showing even white teeth. He said 'You boys had better come with us.'

Hannibal's draw was a thing of wonder. The big man blinked into the barrel of the Colt, blinked again at its twin held in the hand of Jim.

There was a movement behind the big man. Both brothers fired. A swarthy waddy tumbled from his horse.

'After you,' said Jim with a grim smile.

And now the big man and his pards were covered by nine guns. The Lannigan clan meant business.

'I don't think we'll be comin' with you, pardner,' said Hannibal, with crushing simplicity.

'We're a leetle particular the company we keep,' said Jim. He had taken a violent dislike to the big handsome yellow-haired waddy. He felt like leaning forward and spitting right between his eyes.

'Turn your hosses an' mosey along the trail in front of us,' ordered Hannibal.

The big man looked murder but he did as he was told.

'Spread out a bit,' snarled Hannibal. 'Or I'll send a coupla slugs among yuh!'

They obeyed with alacrity leaving their leader in the centre of the trail, his broad back a perfect target.

Jim had no illusions; he knew that if the big man made a false move Hannibal would fill that back full of lead. Not that he wouldn't himself if it came to that! There was something about the big ramrod that got in his craw.

He was still trying to figure out who the big man reminded him of. Or maybe he had seen him some place before. He asked Hannibal softly if he had.

'I don't think so,' said Hannibal. 'If I had I guess I'd remember him. Although when I first saw him he did

59

look kinda familiar.' He raised his voice. 'Hey, big feller! Fall back here.'

The big man turned his head. Hannibal beckoned him with a jerk of his gun. The other stopped his horse and let his men pass him.

'What yuh want?'

'What's your moniker?'

'Hank Meltzer. Why?'

'Have you ever seen any of us before?'

'No. You're all strangers to me. What are yuh doin' around here?'

'I'm askin' the questions,' snarled Hannibal ... 'Are you ramroding this Wagon Wheel spread?'

'Yeh.'

'Who's your boss?'

'His name's Joe Haffer.'

'Too bad we can't stay tuh pay him a visit.'

'Mebbe yuh will,' said Hank Meltzer. He was too cocky; he put them on their guard.

It was Jim who spotted the other riders first. 'Young Hawk-Eye', Hannibal called him. These others were a sizeable length away but coming fast.

'Take these jaspers' guns,' said Hannibal. He raised his voice. 'Easy now. Stand still. Any false moves an' we'll shoot tuh kill.'

Jim and Ep went around and relieved them of their armoury, sharing it out among their own men. They drew away to the side of the trail.

'Turn your hosses,' ordered Hannibal. 'Face 'em the way we came.'

Grins appeared on the faces of the men of the Circle Star. They realized Hannibal's intentions. They raised their guns. Hank Meltzer and his men were lined up now the other way round. The oncoming riders were getting nearer.

There was no time to waste. Hannibal gave an ear-splitting shriek and fired at the heels of the horses. The others

60

followed suit with commendable exuberance. Results were all that could be expected. Two horses backed and unseated their riders. Jim Lannigan had the satisfaction of seeing the yellow-haired ramrod rolling in the dust. His black stallion was a real spirited beast. Riderless, he led the others in a frenzied gallop down the trail.

'Let's git out of here,' said Hannibal. 'We don't want tuh start a range war. Particularly now the odds are about four to one.'

Looking back over his shoulder Jim Lannigan saw Hank Meltzer, now on his feet, gesticulating madly, waving the pursuers on.

But the pursued already had too big a start. A few parting shots speeded them on their way, falling far short of their mark.

Almost an hour later the Circle Star bunch reined in at a little cantina on the edge of the desert. It was called Jose's Joint. The barrel-like Mexican who greeted them with a beaming grin was doubtless Jose in person.

The men washed in buckets outside against the 'dobe wall of the cantina while Jose, helped, or hindered, by his equally fat wife and fat youthful son, prepared their meals. And what meals! A sight for the eyes of hungry and thirsty men. Succulent steaks, done rare like every hard-riding ranny likes them. The inevitable beans, acceptable for all that. Spanish *frjioles* oozing with syrup. Yams and sweetbreads. And quarts of hot black coffee to drink until it dripped from their pores.

Then, everything mopped up, the 'makings' were produced, quirlies rolled, and they leaned back to speculate and chortle.

Hannibal called Jose to him.

'You certainly know how to feed a man,' he said.

'I am glad,' said the Mexican simply. He grinned, showing broken white teeth. 'The practice – eet makes perfect. No?'

'Yes,' said Hannibal; then, seemingly casual, 'You get

61

plenty o' riders along here then although it seems quiet.'

'Pretty well,' said the Mexican. 'I have my regular customers. Jose Joint eet ees a rendezvous. People meet here. Everybody roun' here knows Jose's Joint.'

' We're strangers round here,' said Hannibal. 'Er – say – do any o' the Wagon Wheel boys ride over here any time?'

'The Wagon Wheel,' echoed the Mexican. Then his face lit up. 'Oh, the Wagon Wheel – eet ees over in the Kyper Flats country, Now an' then I see some of their boys – but not ver' often.'

'D'yuh know Hank Meltzer, the foreman?'

'A beeg yeller-haired *hombre*?'

'That's him.'

Jose shrugged. 'I don't know heem much. He's been in here a few times, that's all.'

'Who's the boss o' the Wagon Wheel?'

'A man named Joe Haffer. I have nevair seen heem. They tell me though he ees one big shot *hombre*. Nobody knows much about him. He guards heemself well.'

'We might be doin' some business with the Wagon Wheel' said Hannibal, by way of explanation.

'Not that I hear anything bad about Meester Haffer,' said Jose uncertainly.

'That's all right,' said Hannibal. 'We don't know him either.'

CHAPTER NINE

Sheriff Walt Eckerton was in Dutch again. He seemed to be mighty unpopular with the Circle Star people lately. And that after scouring the country with a posse until his plump flesh was burning with saddle-soreness and he ached in every limb. True, he hadn't found Clem and Bessie Lannigan, or the rustlers, or the stolen cattle – not even one solitary calf. But the Lannigans didn't even seem to think he had tried.

Abel Cornford had been in town again. He said the sheriff hadn't even got an inkling about who killed Bull Kinsell. Walt said he was convinced that Corny Macintosh had done it. What proof had he? Why, there was the money. They hadn't even been able to find out whether the money had belonged to Bull in the first place, Abel told him. Corny must've got it some other way. But that didn't make him a murderer. And where was that money? If the sheriff hadn't succeeded in proving the money was stolen, he'd better give it back to Abel. Abel said he'd make enquiries himself. Maybe Corny had some relatives who were in need of that money. But it was evidence, protested the sheriff.

'Evidence, hell!' snorted Abel. 'Give it over. I guess I don't trust you with a wad like that floating around loose.'

'I don't like your insinuations,' said the sheriff with injured dignity.

'Quit bawlin', Walt,' said the Circle Star foreman with a

63

grin. 'I know yuh too well to be hazin' yuh.'

With a resigned shrug of his massive shoulders the sheriff lumbered to his desk and got the money.

'Yuh understand, Abel,' he said. 'If I prove that young Macintosh did do the job I want it back.'

'Certainly,' said Abel, still grinning. 'How much time do I have tuh give yuh?'

Sheriff Eckerton was too disgusted to answer this one. He snorted as the door closed behind Abel.

Once outside the foreman's face sobered. It was kinda difficult to get really wild with the fat slob. He just never ought to have got to be sheriff, that's all. Still, there was no denying he had had a posse out looking all day yesterday. And there was still a bunch out now under the leadership of his deputy.

Abel was worried. He tried not to contemplate the many terrible things that might have happened to Clem and Bessie. Particularly the girl. Clem, he was a Lannigan. He was tough. He could look out for himself. But the girl. She was a mere kid.

Abel felt savage with a great sense of frustration. So much time wasted and so little done. But what could be done other than what was already being done? To his grief he couldn't answer that question. He felt suddenly old and helpless. He was tough . . . but he'd kind of had a soft spot for them two kids . . . he'd get back to the ranch. Something might've turned up.

Beulah Lannigan came down the house-steps and made for the cookhouse. Her son Jim was just mounting his horse outside the door.

'I'm going a-riding, Ma,' he said. 'I might not be back tonight.'

'Where yuh goin'?' she demanded harshly.

'I don't rightly know. Just a-looking.' Jim kneed his horse forward. When he passed the corral his mother was still talking. He did not look back. He set his horse at a jog-trot.

64

It was almost noon when he passed behind Jose's Joint. He did not want the fat Mexican to see him. Anyway he was all right for grub. His saddle-bag was full of gleanings from the cookhouse.

As he rode his mind was puzzled and disturbed. Although the rest of the boys had dismissed the Wagon Wheel ranch as another empire of an egotistical power maniac not unlike their own boss, he was not satisfied. He thought there was something fishy about the Wagon Wheel. Perhaps it was just prejudice brought about by his sudden unnaturally violent dislike of the yellow-haired ramrod, Hank Meltzer, whose handsome face nagged at his memory. If only he could place it!

He made a detour around the Wagon Wheel territory. Poring over a map of this district yesterday he had come across the name of a railhead town called, flamboyantly, Marlborough Junction.

He figured this place shouldn't be very far past the ranch.

He hit a rough sunken road. This was bound to lead some place. He kept to it.

A minor cloud of dust bearing down on him caused him to draw his mount to the side of the road and wait. Nearer the dust dissolved into a horse and buggy driven by a genial-looking bespectacled fat man in a huge wide-awake hat.

'Hey!' yelled Jim. He waved his hand.

The equipage skidded to a stop, raising more dust. The fat man peered warily through his thick-lensed spectacles. Jim noticed that one plump hand caressed the Winchester on the seat beside him.

Jim grinned and held up his palm in salute.

'Peace, friend,' he said.

The fat man grinned back. 'What can I do for you, young man?'

'Am I on the right road for Marlborough Junction?'

'Yuh shore are,' intoned the fat man. 'You're talkin' to

Doc Rankin, official medico of Marlborough Junction. If you want advice or medicine to alleviate an' ease pain an' ills of the flesh, I'm your man.'

'Thanks, Doc, I'll remember that. Mebbe I'll see yuh again, although preferably not in your – er – official capacity. *Adios*.'

'*Adios*.' The Doc waved expansively and urged his horse on with a jerk of the reins and a click of his tongue. Watching him go Jim reflected sardonically that maybe he was needed in his 'official' capacity at the Wagon Wheel. He was making that way.

Jim discovered the road led him right into the main street of a sizeable town. To the right of him he spotted the gleaming ribbons of a railway-track. Doubtless he was now entering Marlborough Junction. It was the usual sight: dried mud deeply rutted by waggon-wheels, pockmarked by horses' hooves. Board walks each side, sagging a little at the most popular points, mostly outside the honky-tonks.

Some of the buildings were of red brick and most of the 'sporting' houses had new flamboyant false-fronts, as befitted a railhead town catering for visitors.

Jim's bandanna was knotted at the front. He turned it round, pulling the triangular part up over his chin. He jerked the brim of his Stetson over his eyes. It would be hard luck if any Wagon Wheel waddy who had seen him the other day should happen to be in town and should see him again, and recognize him.

First of all he wanted a hot meal. He had eaten all the grub he swiped from the cookhouse earlier on the trail. He spotted a glaringly yellow false-fronted place with a black sign that announced 'The Superb Restaurant.' Jim had his doubts. Nevertheless he dismounted outside there. He tied his mare to the hitching-rack with a feed-bag strapped to her nose.

The Superb Restaurant had double-doors with frosted glass top panels, quite ritzy. The interior, however, had an uncarpeted board-floor. The tables were the usual round plain deal, grease-spotted and ash-bestrewed. The seating accommodation was varied and nondescript.

Jim was accosted by a little fat Mexican, not unlike the proprietor of Jose's Joint. Maybe it was his brother. Jim ordered the usual steak and accessories. Nothing like steak to fill a man out. It was cheap, too. Pat Lannigan didn't pay his men a great wage – his sons got the same as the rest. Anyway, cowpunching wasn't a lucrative profession even in the best circles. That was why there were so many 'nesters' hated by most big ranchers, mushrooming all over the West. A man liked to be independent – even if he was working his guts out on a homestead.

Thinking of homesteads brought his mind around once more to the recurring mystery of the whereabouts of Clem and Bessie. Over his meal he worried the question for the hundredth or so time. But pondering did not get him anywhere.

Halfway through his steak and still deep in his thoughts he was suddenly vaguely aware that somehow all was not right. He looked up at the ornate silver buckle of a gunbelt around the broad flat waist of a hombre standing on the other side of the small table. And beside that another less ornate gunbelt around another gent's waist. And the other side yet another gunbelt. He was ringed by men with gunbelts – businesslike appendages not worn for pleasure. His gaze travelled higher and stopped at the brown handsone face and golden hair of Hank Meltzer.

While he inwardly cursed himself for not keeping his wits about him, Jim kept his eyes level, his voice steady.

'Howdy, stranger,' he said.

'I'm no stranger to you, younker,' retorted Meltzer. 'You've got a nerve coming back here after murdering one of my men.'

So that was the game, was it?

Jim's thoughts were swift; he acted swifter! He jerked his knees up under the table and heaved. Meltzer had been waiting for something like that. He stepped back and grinned. Jim instinctively knew why and, as he rose, he turned. But not quick enough! Something exploded on his head with sickening force. The half-familiar face with the yellow hair was grinning at him as he sank into black nothingness.

When he regained consciousness his first impression was that he was being jolted about unnecessarily. Beneath his nose was the pungent familiar smell of horses. His face was buried in a horse's mane. He straightened up. He was on his own mare, his legs tied to her flanks, his hands tied behind him. Before him was the familiar broad back of Hank Meltzer – only this time Jim had no levelled gun to cover it. There was a man each side of him and he sensed rather than heard the two riding behind him.

Jim felt rather sick. His head throbbed. His voice was hoarse as he shouted 'Hey! Where're yuh taking me?'

Meltzer turned and grinned. His teeth were white and even. He was a handsome bastard! 'You'll find out,' he said.

They were crossing the range now, lush grass swishing round their horse's legs, following no trail – but Meltzer obviously knew where he was heading.

Probably a short cut to the Wagon Wheel ranch, Jim thought. Though why they were taking him there he could not figure. If they really wanted him for the murder of that greaser the other day, they ought to have handed him over to the law at Marlborough Junction.

Pretty soon, however, he saw the sunken road he had travelled that morning, winding below them. Evidently this was just a short cut to the road.

But Meltzer stopped before they reached the road.

Stopped beneath a tall half-withered cotton-wood. Stopped beneath a convenient overhead limb. Only then did Jim realize the yellow-haired man's designs. But he kept his mouth shut.

'Back the hoss under here, headin' away from the road,' Meltzer ordered his men.

68

Two of them, one on each side, caught hold of the bridle of Jim's mare and led her so that his head was directly beneath the bough. With a vicious swing of his arm Meltzer knocked the young cowboy's hat from his head.

Meanwhile one of his men was making a deadly efficient-looking loop in his riata. He slung this over the bough. Jim flinched as the noose caught him a stinging slap across the mouth.

He licked dry lips and said: 'Don't you ever give a man a trial in these parts?'

'Not bushwhackers like you!'

'Bushwhacker, hell! Your greaser was the bushwhacker. Anyway, I didn't shoot him.'

'You'll do.' Meltzer grinned, pleased with his own cynical wit.

One of his men rode forward to place the noose around Jim's neck. Jim acted – his horse bounded forward at a pressure of his knees. Meltzer forestalled the move, blocking the mare's passage. There was a flurry as his men closed around their victim. Meltzer cursed savagely, swinging his arm. His fist caught the younker on the side of the head. Jim swayed but the ropes around his legs and the mare's flanks prevented him from falling.

He shook his head vigorously. His eyes blazed with a murderous light as he looked at Meltzer and cursed him. The big ramrod hit him again across the mouth. Jim spat blood at him.

'Get him under there again,' said Meltzer, grinning savagely. 'Get that necktie around his pipe.'

They did not take any more chances but clustered round the younker, forcing him beneath the tree. A tall jasper with a thatch of ginger hair reached up with the noose. Then he jumped as a slug nearly took his hat off. The report came from the road. Like puppetry all guided by one string, all heads turned in that direction.

Doc Rankin, the fat medico, of Marlborough Junction,

stood up in his buggy, his rifle at his shoulder.

'You know me,' he said affably. 'I never miss. I could've put that slug in Ginger's brain if I'd wanted to. But the next jasper who makes a move'll get it plumb centre. Just tuh make sure I'll have to ask you all to elevate your paws.'

Slowly, reluctantly, all hands went up.

'Don't horn in where you're not wanted, Doc,' said Hank Meltzer. 'This younker killed Pete Margolies an' we aim to make him pay for it.'

'I'm sorry tuh disappoint yuh, Doc,' said Jim, grinning wryly. 'But I didn't have the pleasure.'

'Never mind, I'd still like tuh shake you by the hand.' He addressed the others again and particularly the ginger-headed ranny. 'Hey you, Ginger! You seemed a right handy cuss a while ago. Jest cut my young friend's bonds.' His hand flashed to his belt, then out, steel glittered and a bowie-knife was imbedded in the soil before the redhead's horse. Gingerly the man leaned from the saddle and took the knife.

'Just move along this way, Ginger,' said Doc with a jerk of his head. 'Don't get in the line of fire . . . now cut the ropes. Easy does it.'

Jim flexed his cramped arms and legs, then reached up and gently removed the noose from around his neck.

'Has anybody got the young man's gunbelt?' said the Doc.

'Here it is across my saddle-horn,' growled Hank Meltzer.

'Give it him . . . easy now, Hank.'

Jim took the gunbelt with a grin at the ramrod's discomfiture. 'Thanks, Hank,' he said. He leaned closer. 'Some day I'm gonna kill you,' he said.

Meltzer showed his teeth in snarl but did not say anything.

'Get back in line, Hank,' said the Doc.

Meltzer did as he was told. Jim joined the medico on the road. 'Thanks, Doc,' he said.

'Forget it, son. Get going – pronto!'

'But how about you?'

'Don't you worry, son, I'll handle Hank Meltzer an' his boys. They won't do me no harm . . . get goin' I say. My arm's beginnin' to ache holdin' this tarnation gun.' The Doc's voice was sharp.

'All right, Doc. Thanks again. I owe you a heap. If ever you're over in the Smoky Range country call on the Circle Star.'

'All right.'

It was, however, with misgivings that Jim galloped away. He looked back in time to see the Doc clambering from his buggy, the rifle still levelled at the erstwhile lynch-party.

CHAPTER TEN

For three days now the bottom of Old Smoky Gulch had been twelve feet deep in billowing mist, the last five feet or so being thicker than 'Greasy' Masters' beans and tomato soup. In the mist, men had searched the rocky surface for traces of Clem and Bessie Lannigan. They groped and stumbled and cursed and found nothing. Now everybody was of the opinion that the rustlers had taken the young couple with them to hold to ransom. There was much speculation. Very few would be sorry to see old Pat gulled, for plenty – providing the younkers came to no harm of course. Some said old Pat was too tight-fisted to pay for the freedom of even his son and daughter-in-law – 'specially as he'd been estranged from them. Jumptown loungers made bets on it.

Then on the fourth day – the very day on which young Jim went a-riding on his lonesome – the bottom of Old Smoky became almost clear. Resolved not to leave a stone unturned, yet very reluctantly it seemed, Hannibal, Kim, Ep and Jonathon descended the tortuous trail to the bottom. There they split up and began to search. For what?

Ep found something first – a small thing unnoticed by other searchers who had blindly groped. His bass voice awoke the echoes eerily as he called to the others.

The mist, now only in swirling patches, lapped round their ankles as they ran to him.

While they gathered around him Ep held in his large hand a knife made all in one piece – the handle was of the same steel as the blade.

'You know what that is, don't yuh?' he said. 'Or what it was, at least.'

The others looked dubious. 'No,' said Jonathon.

'A cold chisel,' Ep told them. 'The one end's bin heated an' flattened out, then filed to a point. The other end – look yuh – you can see it's a chisel – it's eight-sided, an' see how the ends bin battered smooth and bent over a little ragged at the edges by blows of a hammer.'

'Yeh, that's it. I can seen it now,' said Hannibal. Kim and Jonathon said they could too.

'I don't know much about such things,' said Kim. 'They ain't used much hereabouts, are they?'

'There's only one place I guess where they could be used,' said Ep.

'The M.L.G. place,' said Jonathon.

'Hum,' said Hannibal. 'But thet don't signify nothin'.' He broke away. 'Stick it in your belt, Ep, an' let's keep on lookin'. You take that side.' He waved an arm. 'An' you, Jonathon, you take the other side. Me an' Kim'll keep in the middle.'

They carried on in silence, clambering over huge boulders that bestrewed the floor of the chasm, dodging fissures in the rocks, now upright, now bending, sometimes on their knees, and often hidden from each others' sight.

A terrible cry from Jonathon, the clan's weakling, brought them all panting to his side. Their eyes followed the direction of his pointing, shaking finger. Ep and Hannibal both blanched visibly but did not speak. Kim staggered as if he had been struck and blasphemed softly.

From behind a cluster of boulders protruded a white, bloodied leg, a woman's slipper half-off a shattered foot, a pitiful fragment of gay skirt across a knee.

The four brothers stood motionless for seconds that

seemed an age to them all. Then something like a sob escaped from Hannibal's set lips and he strode forward.

He said 'I – I guess none o' the search parties came this far, 'cause they was scairt o' stumbling into a fissure while the mist was on.'

It needed a commonplace remark lie that to jerk the other three from their horrified trance. They followed him. Behind the battered body of his wife, and completely hidden by the rocks was the corpse of Clem Lannigan. Both bodies had been riddled with bullets.

Quickly, silently, and with eyes averted as much as possible from their pitiful burdens the brothers carried the bodies up the tortuous trail to the top of Old Smoky.

'They must've jest took 'em to the lip an' then shot 'em,' said Hannibal.

'Whoever did it we'll make them pay,' said Kim hoarsely. 'We'll make them pay.'

Jim Lannigan arrived home just behind the melancholy cavalcade. He found his father raving like a maniac, his mother a strange, strain-faced woman with grief and murder parked in her eyes. He viewed the remains with mingled horror, and pity, and with cold hate, vowing like his brother to make somebody pay. A few short days ago this had been a laughing bride, and that a young man with worlds to conquer. His brother and his best friend, and a girl he had thought to help and protect like a sister. But away with sentiment! There was a lot to be done.

Ep's finding of the chisel cum-knife quite close to the murdered couple had determined old Pat once and for all that the M.L.G. people were to blame for everything. He was calling most of the men in from the range. Everybody wasn't as certain as he, but they wanted blood. They would follow the old man wherever he led them.

Pretty soon a hundred or so horsemen were milling in the yard. Old Pat came out of the ranch-house door and down the veranda steps. Beulah followed him across the veranda and stayed on the top of the steps, watching. Her hands were lax in front of her, folded on her apron, her face was grim.

A young ranny brought Pat's horse to him and he mounted. He took his place at the head of his men, Hannibal, Ep, Kim, Jonathon, and Jim ranged themselves alongside him. The rest formed a rough column behind them.

Old Pat did not speak. He just put spurs to his horse. For a moment he was in front of the rest. Then his sons caught up with him. The rest streamed behind.

Beulah watched them until they were a mere cloud of dust upon the range. Then she turned and went back into the house.

Mancy Carter had planted a guard on top of a flat-roofed tool-shed on the edge of the M.L.G. camp. There a man squatted on a bale of straw with a rifle across his knees. From his perch he could see all the surrounding range.

He saw the oncoming riders and gave the warning by firing his gun in the air. Both Mancy Carter and his *segunda* Pete Listery, ran across to him. Carter shinned up the ladder that was leaning against the shed wall and joined the guard on the roof.

He shaded his eyes with his hands. 'The Circle Star bunch,' he said. He called down to his second in command 'Pete, get all the men across here. Leave about half-a-dozen of 'em at the back – just in case.'

With almost panicky haste Listery scuttled off to do as he was bid.

The beating of hammers ceased and the men began to congregate on the edge of the camp.

'Spread out,' bawled Carter from his perch. 'Take cover. Make sure you've got plenty ammunition and guns.' He spoke to the guard and they both climbed down.

The straw-haired Irishman, Callahan, was much in evidence now, bullying the men to their places, doing more to help than Pete Listery, who was running around

75

like a prairie-dog with his tail shot off.

It was Hannibal Lannigan who halted the attackers with a motion of his huge hand. Old Pat cursed. 'What's the idea?'

'They've seen us,' said Hannibal.

'They shore have,' said Kim. 'Look at 'em. They're all out front there an' takin' cover.'

'I suggest we fan out,' said Jim.

'Good idea, younker,' agreed Ep. Hannibal rose up in his stirrups and turned.

'Break up an' fan out,' he yelled. 'Keep low on your hosses' backs. It looks like they've got us covered. If any of yuh wants tuh drop out now's your chance.'

Nobody took advantage of the offer. Pat and his sons had their heads together. Abel Cornford joined up with them. Hannibal stood up again. He bawled 'We're gonna split up into three groups. Me an' Dad'll take the middle one, Ep an' Jim another one, an' Abel and Kim the other.' It was significant that he left out brother Jonathon, who was definitely not a fighting man. 'When I fire my gun in the air we charge!' concluded Hannibal.

For a moment the range was a stamping, dusty mêlée of men and horses. Then the men were in their groups, spread out in a wide half-circle with a gap between each group. The group each end expected to swing round before the middle one and take the M.L.G. camp on each flank.

Mancy Carter had spotted the manoeuvre and was replacing his men. Hannibal gave the signal to the attackers: if they could get in while the defenders were still in flux they had an even chance. Many of the riders could not but admit in their own minds, however, that the M.L.G. people looked the stronger force – and they also had the advantage of cover.

At the camp men were still scurrying about. Their first volley was ragged and very unsuccessful, the only casualty being one Circle Star horse. The attackers, most of whom had toted guns since they were kids realised that there were very few marksmen among the M.L.G. workers.

The gap was very narrow . . . then on the left flank, the group led by Abel and Kim broke through the barriers. Next moment the whole of the Circle Star were there and it was hand-to-hand fighting. And at this the M.L.G. men were on their mettle. They attacked with picks, shovels, hammers and other queer miscellaneous articles none the less deadly. By tacit unspoken agreement on both sides there was no more shooting. The Circle Star men, in traditional Western style, used their guns as clubs, used their fists, their boots, their spurs. They'd show these 'Micks' and Eastern scum. . . ! But alas, they were outnumbered, flustered by a veritable storm of big Irishmen, lithe Italians with all the tricks of the Bowery, Swedes, Germans, Mexicans, half-castes, and even Chinamen. None of the milling men noticed Jonathon Lannigan galloping his horse madly away from the scene of combat – or if they did they had no time to stop and comment of the fact.

Kim Lannigan went down, his head gashed by a blow from a hammer wielded by a little dark man about half the size of himself. Big Ep was swapping blow for blow with the indefatigable Callahan, and only just managing to hold his own. Huge Hannibal had two men on his hands. One of them, a slinky half-breed, drew a knife. Hannibal kicked it out of his hand, feeling the wrist bone crunch beneath the heavy toe of his boot. The man screamed shrilly. Then Hannibal's hamlike fist to the side of his head put an end to his agony. The other assailant, a big Nordic-looking type, swung at Hannibal with a shovel. The big Lannigan brother grunted as the sharp blade bit into his side. Then, before the man could strike again, he had closed in and had his hands around his throat. He squeezed until the man went limp, then let him slump to the ground like a sack of meal. He turned swiftly to meet another attacker.

Abel Cornford went down beneath the weight of a young Italian who was intent on braining him with a hammer. As he raised the weapon for the finishing blow, young Jim Lannigan kicked him in the back of the neck and he was catapulted from Abel to settle in an inert heap a few feet away.

Jim helped the foreman to his feet and side by side they met the attack of two more husky specimens. As Jim closed with the biggest of the two he saw his dad a little way away floor a huge ginger-haired bully. The old man could certainly look after himself. . . ! A brawny knee in his groin made Jim gasp and double-up. On his knees, with sickness welling up inside him he forgot all about his Dad. He saw a heavy boot approaching his face at lightning speed, and instinctively threw his hands up, throwing himself back-wards at the same time as he grasped and pulled. His assailant landed beside him. The next moment they were locked in each others arms like a loving couple.

Being the first down Jim had a little advantage. He took it and was pretty soon on top dealing sledge-hammer blows to the others face. Flesh and blood, no matter how husky, could not stand this for long and with a strangled sigh the M.L.G. man closed his eyes and subsided.

Jim rose to his feet. With his back to him another M.L.G. character had just swiped murderously with a pick at a Circle Star waddy. Luckily he missed. Jim drew his gun and slapped the man over the head with the barrel. One point of the pick stuck in the soil as it was dropped. The other point punctured the man's shoulder as he fell on it.

'Thanks, Jim,' said the waddy.

Jim nodded, turning, looking for Abel. He was just in time to see the foreman floor his man with a beautiful uppercut. Plenty o' life in the old dog yet!

Abel strode over the prostrate body of his opponent and joined Jim and the other younker. Before them was a milling free-for-all. They threw themselves into it with gusto. And at that moment a shot rang out.

It was like a signal. Men paused in their fighting, looked round to see who had fired the shot. Whether it was a

Circle Star or M.L.G. man, men's hands went to their belts. Lives hung in the balance. It could mean murder – carnage! Then somebody spotted the bunch of horsemen coming across the range and shouted:

'The sheriff! A posse!'

Fat Walt Eckerton never knew how many lives he had saved that sunny afternoon. But looking very relieved beside him was Jonathon, the weakling of the Lannigan clan. Then he saw his Dad who had been hurt by a stray bullet and ran to him. Old Pat cursed and spat at him before he passed out.

CHAPTER ELEVEN

The identity of the gunman who shot old Pat remained a mystery. When questioned by the sheriff the M.L.G. men were irritatingly obtuse and none of their erstwhile opponents had seen a thing. They had been the attackers and, either way, Eckerton couldn't do much about the ruckus. Mancy Carter, who hadn't been seen since he descended from the look-out right at the beginning of the mêlée, mysteriously re-appeared and waxed highly indignant at the Circle Star's unprovoked attack. The fact, however, that Pat Lannigan was the only person seriously injured, sort of evened things up a bit; a rather bewildered sheriff shrugged his plump shoulders and left it at that.

The Circle Star mob, carrying their wounded leader with them, set out for home. Without old Pat's rage and convictions to spur them on, they felt rather depleted. Anyway, the cosmopolitan labouring men they had been fighting didn't seem to have the makings of accomplished rustlers.

Sheriff Eckerton and his posse drew in their horns and meandered back to Jumptown. The M.L.G. men began to clear the mess up. So ended the battle of Smoky Range.

Many of the Circle Star men, Jim and Hannibal Lannigan among them, were almost beginning to think that weak brother Jonathon had done a good thing in fetching a posse – if the law had not arrived when it did there might have been terrible bloodshed with consequences beyond contemplation. And, after all, there was still no actual proof that Mancy Carter or any of his men had anything to do with the rustling or the murder of Bessie and Clem – despite Ep Lannigan's finding of the chisel-cum-knife by the bodies. Once more the Circle Star mob had been led into battle by their firebrand employer. Though it must be admitted that most of them enjoyed fighting – they had been hired for that reason.

Right now Jim Lannigan was savage with himself for once more blindly following his father. It proved that the old man still had a subtle power over him – more power maybe than Jim cared to admit, even to himself. He ought to have asked questions first, thought things over. Not that he condoned Jonathon's sneaking away to fetch the law. He had probably thought more about his own skin than anything else – he'd always had a yellow streak.

All the time Jim had been skittling members of the M.L.G. combine, his subconscious mind had been working overtime for him. And it had at last solved one little problem – partly, at least. And also given him just the beginning of a theory.

He contemplated taking Hannibal into his confidence. The big man's simple mind had a happy knack of discarding all but essentials. Maybe he'd be able to sort the grain from the chaff. Maybe . . .

Old Pat, whose wound had been roughly bandaged by Abel Cornford, regained consciousness before they reached the ranch-house, and began to curse hoarsely, calling them 'yeller skunks' (and worse) and exhorting them to turn back and show the M.L.G. scum who was master of Smoky Range. Although Abel gently explained to him that the law had stepped in he would not be pacified. Walt Eckerton was 'an idle, ignorant clod' – 'he wouldn't punish the murderers of Bessie and Clem.' Old Pat was in the grips of an obsession, common to ruthless egotists of his type and intensified in this case by his feverish condition.

Beulah Lannigan received them in silence and commanded her sons to put their father, who was now mumbling incoherently, to bed. She said she could handle things all right – Pat had had worse wounds than that in his day. Nevertheless, unbeknown to his implacable mother, young Jim changed horses and rode into Jumptown for a doctor.

Benjamin Millership, Jumptown's only medico was a harsh, unfriendly beanpole of a man in late middle age, so unlike, Jim reflected, the genial good Samaritan of Marlborough Junction, Doc Rankin. Doctor Millership (never 'Doc') however, was a good medico. He lived with his only daughter, Arrabella, just the two of them (his wife had left him years ago) in a large frame house on the outskirts of the cowtown. He was an unusual type to come across in a little cowtown, not a 'mixer' and pretty brilliant really. He had been there as long as the town had – almost twenty-nine years; maybe some scandal had driven him away from the usual haunts of such men as he. Maybe he had good reasons to be harsh, unfriendly and intolerant. He carried a short, twin-barrelled derringer in his hip-pocket and he knew how to use it. Boot Hill nursed the remains of more than one man who had gotten too fresh with Doctor Benjamin Millership. He had proved that he was as proficient and cold-blooded in taking life as he was in saving it.

Arrabella Millership, twenty-six years old and so like her father in looks and disposition, so obviously doomed to dried up spinsterhood, opened the door to Jim Lannigan and told him her father was out on a case. Jim asked her to tell him when he returned to make speed to the Circle Star. She gave him her promise with a vinegary smile. Poor gal, thought Jim inconsistently, and contrasted her with the radiant Bessie who had been so foully murdered. He felt sad and frustrated. He went into the Jolly Moses to get a drink, resolving that later he would call at the doctor's again just in case any slip-ups occurred.

The saloon was full; among the gathering Jim recognized members of Eckerton's erstwhile posse. It was pretty obvious what the main topic of conversation was right now. Many voices greeted Jim; some asked about old Pat. Jim told them as much as he could about his father's condition, but gave the impression he didn't want to be questioned further. He knew he wasn't really unpopular himself – but his Dad certainly was. He figured that about half, if not more, of the company were M.L.G. sympathizers. They gloried in hearing of old Pat's tumble from his high horse. Not that he hadn't asked for it, the old man's son reflected sardonically.

He ordered a drink at the bar and took it to a small table in a corner. Strangely enough nobody bothered him. He sat alone.

He gulped his first beer. Gosh, he had certainly needed that. He went to the bar and fetched another one, returning to the table with it. And still he sat alone.

He that sitteth alone . . . what had Clem used to say? Clem had been an educated cuss for a cowhand. Read a good many books when he was a kid. . . . His thoughts kept returning to Clem and Bessie. He certainly missed 'em. If he could get the snake who . . . a slight commotion in the crowd drew his attention, interrupting his thoughts.

A dirty, straw-thatched head, battered hat on the back of it, hove in view, and two piggy eyes looked at Jim. Behind Callahan were four or five of his cronies. Callahan came out of the crowd, came nearer to Jim. His mates followed him. Jim noted the big Irishman didn't wear a gun, leastways not in sight anyway, but at least three of the others were armed. Callahan waited until these others were with him, until they also had seen Jim. As if by a signal everybody else moved further back.

Jim braced himself. He grinned up one side of his mouth. There was no mirth behind his grin. It seemed like every time he entered a saloon lately he ran into trouble. And Callahan by the looks of things certainly meant trouble.

Then the big Irishman swore, the curses sounded queer

in his thick Irish brogue, He started forward. That was all
the provocation Jim needed. He leapt to his feet, kicking
the small table over with a clatter. He was no slouch on the
draw. Callahan gaped at the barrel of a forty-five.

One of the men behind Callahan went for his gun. Jim
fired. The man squealed and clutched his forearm. His
gun clattered to the floor. It was a fast draw. Jim was
surprised. He hadn't thought any of 'em would be that
handy.

He now held the whip-hand. Nobody else seemed
inclined to make a move.

'Rush him, bhoys,' said Callahan, but his voice lacked
verve, and he didn't venture to lead the way. He hardly
moved a muscle.

Jim knew, however, that he could not trust his luck
indefinitely. He was a bit leery of M.L.G. sympathizers in
the crowd. Slowly he skirted the fallen table.

'Back over there,' he barked at Callahan and his
cronies. He jerked his head in the direction of the bar.
They backed away, the wounded man still clutching his
bloodied arm, his face a sickly yellow.

At this juncture a diversion occurred. Pierre Flaubin
stepped suddenly into the cleared space, a pearl-handled
revolver in each hand. He covered both Jim and the opposite bunch.

'All right, Jeem,' he said. 'Put your gun away. I'll take
over from now on. You'd better vamoose.'

Jim shrugged and holstered his weapon. 'All right,
Pierre,' he said. Then he spoke directly to Callahan. 'If
you want to follow this up, big boy, I'll meet you in the
street in half-an-hour's time. Guns, fists, or anything you
like to choose.'

'Oi'll be there, me bhoy,' said the big Irishman.

The onlookers parted to let Jim through; a few of them
slapped his shoulders in approbation as he passed them.
He left the saloon and made tracks again for Doctor
Millership's place. Arrabella opened the door to him once

84

more, and told him that the doctor had been home and was already on his way to the Circle Star. Jim thanked her and left.

From there he went to the livery-stables to see old Jeb Crockett, father of the tragic Bessie. Maybe there was some little thing he could do. The Crocketts lived over the top of the stables.

Jeb was sitting alone in his little cubb-hole. Awkwardly Jim offered his condolences.

'I know, Jim,' said the old man. 'Yuh don't have tuh say any more.'

'How's Mrs Crockett?'

'Purty sick, I guess, Jim. Aunt Mab's in there with her. I left 'em together an' came out here for a piece. I'm kinda muddled, Jim. Who could've . . .' his voice trailed off into a murmur. Twice his lips framed his daughter's name, but the words seemed to stick in his throat.

Jim was inarticulate before this stoical, painful grief. If he had the man. . . ! Maybe Callahan . . . no, he didn't think so somehow, although quite possibly he had something to do with it.

He pressed the old man's shoulder and without another word turned and left.

The half-hour was nearly up. He strolled down the middle of the street towards the Jolly Moses. The street was deserted. He went in 'Curly' Wallin's barbershop opposite the saloon. The little plump middle-aged barber with the puff-ball mop of black hair that earned him his nickname, was a special friend of Jim's.

He had already heard of the impending fight. 'Watch him, Jim,' he said. 'He looks treacherous.' He jerked a thumb at a shotgun in a corner. 'Just in case, I'll be watching with li'l Horace there.'

Jim was raring to go; his only speculation was about Callahan's choice of weapons – if any. Bitter rage was burning inside him and he meant to take some of it out on somebody. Why not the cocky Irishman?

He sat in a barber's chair and looked out of the window at the batwings of the saloon opposite. Waiting made him more savage; he strove to remain cool. His wait was not long.

The batwings swung open and disgorged the rag, tag and bobtail of Jumptown, among them Callahan and his cronies. They spread out, some on the side-walks, others in groups across the street, forming a rough arena. For a moment Jim lost sight of Callahan. Then he saw him again as he swaggered to the middle of the street. He had discarded his gunbelt. Elation seized Jim. He felt like whooping. So it was to be in the raw! That was the way he felt too.

Curly slapped his back as he rose to his feet. 'You can take him, Jimmy,' he said.

Then Jim opened the door and stepped out on to the sidewalk.

'Here he is,' somebody yelled.

The two contestants grinned mirthlessly at each other. Without undue haste Jim removed his gunbelt. A man stepped forward. A man whom Jim liked, a half-pint sized odd-jobber called Luke Higgins. Jim gave Luke the belt and gun.

Callahan removed his hat, waistcoat and scarf, and tossed them back to his pards. Jim did likewise and gave his to Luke. Then he strode forward to meet Callahan.

CHAPTER TWELVE

Doctor Millership, clad in tight black clothes, always rode a large, black raw-boned stallion. Horse and rider were well suited: to see them prancing majestically across a skyline was an awe-inspiring sight. For such a prominent-boned animal the black was some galloper. The doctor sat him straight, a pipe-stem figure crowned by a dark wide-awake.

The loping stallion ate up the miles between Jumptown and the Circle Star. Its rider had his bag on the saddle before him, holding it with one hand, his other loosely holding the reins. He kept perfect balance. Horse and rider had been together so long that they were now like compact, well-oiled machinery.

Down the little-used trail to the unpopular Circle Star ranch, horse and rider overtook a little plump man in a buggy drawn by a grey mare. They were about to pass when the plump man called 'Excuse me, my friend.'

Millership turned his head and although his face did not lose its usual stern expression, he obligingly reined in to a jog-trot, pulling nearer to the buggy.

'Am I on the right road to the Circle Star ranch?' queried the little plump man.

'You certainly are, sir,' was the courteous, though wholly disinterested reply. 'I am on my way there myself and would willingly escort you the rest of the way – but I am a doctor: a patient awaits me there, and I must make haste.'

The other man's plump, pleasant visage creased in a smile. He matched the other's old-world manner with his own. He said:

'An agreeable coincidence, friend. I, too, am a doctor. Doctor Rankin, late of Marlborough Junction, at your service, sir.'

For a moment a faint glimmer of interest, maybe a sign of agreeable surprise, lightened the other's grim countenance. It passed and he said:

'How do you do. I am Doctor Millership of Jumptown. May I ask whether your visit to the Circle Star is concerned at all with my patient, Mr Pat Lannigan?'

'It is not,' replied Doc Rankin. 'I don't know Mr Pat Lannigan. I was invited there by a young man, Mr Jim Lannigan.'

'Ah, Pat Lannigan's youngest son,' said Doctor Millership. 'I am very much afraid you may not find young Jim at home, unless he has gone in front of me. I'm inclined to think, however, he has stayed behind in Jumptown. Nevertheless,' he added. 'I should not let Jim's absence deter you. If you are a friend of his, you will be very welcome at the Circle Star.'

'I shall press on then,' said Doc Rankin. 'And if I can be of any assistance . . .' he paused.

Doctor Millership said magnanimously, 'I may need your help, Doctor. If so, I shall certainly take advantage of your generous offer.'

'We of the profession must stick together,' said Doc Rankin, sententiously, but there was a twinkle in his eyes. 'However, Doctor Millership, do not let me keep you – I can get along under my own steam.'

'I will carry on then,' said the other. 'And will acquaint the Circle Star of your impending arrival.'

He bowed gravely. At a touch from his heels the big black bounded forward. They went down the trail like a cannonball wreathed in smoke. Doc Rankin whistled shrilly between his teeth.

'That's made you jealous, ain't it, you ol' warhorse,' he said to his mare. 'Giddup there!'

In those days of the West when most fights were speedily ended by flying lead, usually with fatal results for one or both of the contestants, fist-fights were pretty rare. And such a battle of giants as the one enacted in the street of Jumptown late on that summer afternoon were a rarity indeed. Twenty years later garrulous old-timers were still telling of it with bated breath, and a wealth of gestures and ferocious facial expressions.

They told of how the big straw-haired Irishman, Callahan, pulled his sweaty shirt over his head and threw it back into the crowd. Of how Jim Lannigan, only twenty, but big and strong, paused in his stride and did likewise. And of how the atmosphere was smoky then with the approaching dusk and the lights were going on in the buildings around as the crowd grew in size.

Callahan was the heavier of the two. His chest, arms and shoulders swelled superbly and were sprinkled with fine golden hairs. But his waist was growing flabby with too much eating, drinking and doubtless, evasion of hard work.

Jim Lannigan was younger by ten years or more but, though as tall, more slenderly built. His shoulders and chest, however, were magnificent, and a slight fuzz of black hairs on the latter. He tapered down to a washboard middle. He was the fitter of the two, but the odds were slightly on the side of the human 'grizzly' who opposed him.

Both men shuffled forward, Jim poised on the balls of his feet, Callahan flat-footed, knees bent, crouching. They circled warily, elbows bent, fingers crooked in a half-boxing, half-wrestling stance. Then Jim's fist clenched, drew back, shot forward at lightning speed. Moving deceptively fast, Callahan caught the blow on his shoulder. Jim's follow-up left whistled beneath the big man's nose. Then Callahan's clutching fingers grasped him. Jim twisted like an eel and was out of danger, but not before the long nails of Callahan's right hand had drawn four crimson grooves down the side of his chest. First blood to the Irishman! A low sibilant murmur came from the crowd.

Callahan went after his man, sliding on flat feet. Jim backed away a little. Callahan rushed. Jim side-stepped. A huge fist grazed his shoulder. Jim lashed out. It was a wild blow but it caught the big Irishman in the chest, stopping him in his tracks with a painful grunt. The shock jolted Jim's arm to his elbow. He stepped sideways to face his man, boring in with both fists. But Callahan was ready for him. They stood toe to toe swapping blows.

The crowd went wild, each man yelling the name of his particular fancy, exhorting him to do this – do that! There seemed almost equal supporters on each side. Pierre Flaubin stood in the forefront of the crowd on the Jolly Moses side of the street. He did not shout at all, but watched the contest with keen eyes, which lit up when a clean blow was struck or a tricky manoeuvre circumvented. He had seen many a mill like this in his youth at the lumber-camps of the south-west.

On the opposite side of the street beside Luke Higgins, with one foot on Jim's clobber, stood the barber, the butt of his shotgun ground in the dust beside him. He had discovered his view was obscured by the people in front of his window so, after closing his shop, wormed his way to the front of the crowd. He meant to see fair play – or else!

Jim was faster on his feet than Callahan – and he needed to be! The big Irishman was throwing punches terrible enough to poleaxe a steer. Jim was gradually going back before him, bobbing and weaving, throwing a retaliating blow now and then, drawing his man on.

'Fight back, yuh young skunk!' yelled one of Callahan's cronies.

Jim grinned through split and swollen lips. Callahan

was enraged: he made another blind rush. That was what the young man had been waiting for. He side-stepped and as Callahan charged past him, hit him with all his might on the side of his jaw. The thwack of the blow was a sickening sound. Callahan pulled up straight, a dazed expression on his bovine face. Then Jim was in front of him, his arms, each one loaded with an iron-like fist, working like pistons. *One – two – three – four – five* . . . and Callahan was down!

The crowd roared. A few of them surged forward.

'Keep back!' barked Pierre Flaubin. 'He's getting up!'

And indeed he was – after a hurricane of blows that would have put an ordinary man down for a long count.

He was on his knees. Then, with a burst of energy, he was on his feet and boring forward, head down. Jim met him. His first blow sought for the big man's midriff, but the follow-up was too eager: it exploded on the top of the other's bullet head. The watchers saw Jim wince.

'I betcha that's busted his hand,' said somebody.

It had not – but it had considerably weakened his wrist. The pain was nauseating. Jim danced away, fighting the weakness off. Callahan had suffered too. He was doubled-up, shaking his head like a wounded bull.

He straightened up as his opponent came towards him again. They circled, their arms waving like tentacles feeling for an opening. The crowd, thirsting for more action, more blood, tried to egg them on with compliments or catcalls as the fancy took them.

There was a commotion in the mob strung across the street, and cries of: 'You keep out o' this, Walt.' 'Nobody's gettin' kilt.' 'Don't start anything, sheriff' 'Go an' boil your fat head' . . . and other choice remarks. Sheriff Eckerton had come to see what all the ruckus was about.

He assured everybody plaintively that if it was a fair and above-board fist-fight he wasn't going to interfere. Grudgingly the ranks moved and he found a place for himself among them.

It was almost dark now. The lights from many open doors and windows were sending their streaming rays across the street, illuminating faces grave and gay, rough, vicious, unshaven, cleanshaven, bearded, homely, ugly, yelling toothless mouths and mouths full of decay; now and then the flashing white teeth of a young cowboy or a girl not yet polluted by cowtown night-life, but who yelled as loud, and was as garishly painted as the middle-aged harridans with whom she congregated. Lust and excitement was on every face; even the laughter had gloating undertones.

Moving across the paths of light, their naked torsos pulsing and glistening with sweat and blood, their faces red-smeared, puffed, hideous as painted braves, the fighters looked like two giant fiends of hell.

They clashed and all laughter and badinage was forgotten as with one mighty voice the crowd yelled hoarsely for blood! Callahan had one mighty arm around the young man's waist, the other bent upwards, the heel of his hand under the young man's chin, pressing his head back, the clutching fingers clawing his face. Jim's fists pummelled frenziedly, but he was too close to do much damage. He was being pressed back – back until it seemed his spine would crack. But as he went back he had more room for his arms, his blows travelled further and faster, exploding against Callahan's already terribly battered face. Jim's face was contorted with agony, his eyes started from his head, sweat poured from him, he punched mechanically, grunting painfully with each blow.

With each blow Callahan's head jerked back on his bull neck. His eyes began to film, his grip slackened, his fingers scrabbled frantically at Jim's face. Then suddenly they parted, both reeling like drunken men.

Jim spread his feet apart to steady himself, gulping in great lungfuls of sweet night air. Phew! that had been a close one. The pain in his back and ribs was excruciating. Callahan was resting his hands on his bent knees, his leonine head thrust forward. His one eye was completely closed, his other a mere dull glimmer: he would carry some of the marks of this experience for the rest of his life. The blood from the fresh wounds on his face ran down his neck and chest.

A man appeared with a lantern and hung it on a nail imbedded in the hitching-post of the Jolly Moses. The stage was set for the last act. Terrible, awe-inspiring. The crowd forgot to yell the names of their favourites. Their gabble died to a murmur. Then to silence. They waited.

Callahan straightened up, blinking in the light, his chest heaving, his arms slightly crooked, his fingers clenching and unclenching.

Jim Lannigan took two shambling paces forward. Callahan followed his example and, even as he did so, the other literally threw himself across the space that separated them. His charge sent Callahan reeling. Jim followed him up, punching now at the roll of flesh around his middle. Callahan went down. Jim's momentum carried him on to him. The crowd went wild. Callahan brought his knee sharply under the young man's chin. Jim was propelled away from him and went down himself.

Both men rose almost simultaneously. They were slower to attack. Both were getting towards the end of their tether, only supermen such as they could stand the pace as long as they had.

They sparred, Callahan's hands, like huge claws, trying to get a grip. Jim, fists bunched trying to get under them to punish that flabby waist some more. A few more blows in the midriff and he figured Callahan was done for. Either that or he himself would be finished. He was feeling mighty weak. If Callahan got those arms of his round his ribs again he'd crack for sure.

The big man's arms became a hoop under which he dodged, driving his fists into Callahan's body with all the strength he had left. Callahan groaned and doubled up, his clutching hands tearing at the flesh of Jim's chest. The crowd heard Callahan's groan answered by a sharp hiss of agony from the other. The crowd was quiet again. The laboured gasps of the contestants were like throbbing pulses of agony in the stillness.

Callahan's one arm was around Jim's body, but he could not get a grip and all the time the other's blows, each one like a ball of fire bursting inside of him, were doubling him up, further snapping his strength and resistance. He bent, and squeezed, taking Jim over with him. Jim's elbows drew back one by one and with his last desperate strength he drove his fists – once – twice.

Callahan sagged forward. Jim went down before him, the other's huge weight pressing him down in the dust. Everything went black. He was in danger of being suffocated. Frenziedly he tried to move the huge bulk. He was weak – like a prairie rabbit. Vaguely he heard the crowd, like the roaring of the great Norther as it came sweeping across the winter ranges. Nearer – nearer . . . then the blackness rolled away and it was light again. Hands helped him to his feet, voices told him he had won. Then he was standing up straight, steadying himself with his hand on someone's shoulder, looking down at the unconscious bulk of Callahan, his straw-coloured hair dirty and matted with blood, his eyes closed, like a grizzly bear, beaten and helpless.

CHAPTER THIRTEEN

'I guess we should be nearly there,' said Doc Rankin, talking to his mare between the shafts.

He certainly hoped they were. It was getting dark, he wanted to reach the Circle Star before it got real black. He didn't want to lose his way. The trail wasn't too clear hereabouts.

That thin, queer *hombre*, Doc Millership, would be there now he figured. He wondered how the patient was faring. He looked behind him. A while ago he thought he saw a rider back there. Well, whoever he was, unless he was just an hallucination, he certainly had vanished.

The Doc looked out front again. 'Giddup there, old gel,' he said.

He was bent forward a little, talking softly to the mare when something hit him with terrific force in the side. Burning, stunning, knocking him from his seat and on to the road. He felt nothing when he hit it. He did not hear the flat report of the rifle.

But the horse heard it; there was no gentle guiding hand on the reins, the beast got scared and bolted.

Doc Rankin lay there in a cushiony tumbled heap, five – ten – fifteen minutes and did not move. Then galloping hooves sounded, coming nearer. A rider appeared in the dusk, coming down the trail from the direction of the Circle Star. He slowed his horse to a canter, looking about him nervously. It was Jonathon Lannigan.

Then he saw the body of the doctor. He started, reined in his horse, looking about him again. He seemed reassured and, riding his horse to the body, dismounted. He grunted as he lifted the little plump bundle across his saddle horn. He climbed up quickly behind it then, with a few more quick looks around set spurs to his mount, and galloped back the way he had come.

When Jim Lannigan, sick and sore and dead beat, arrived home late that night he learned that his Dad was quiet and sleeping, and that Doctor Millership had returned to Jumptown after promising to call again the following day. He also heard that a mysterious stranger, a little fat *hombre*, had been discovered wounded beside the trail and was lying unconscious in the spare room.

Millership had already gone by the time Jonathon arrived with his burden, so old Abel Cornford had done the best he could and was now sitting-up at the stranger's bedside. Jonathon said the Jumptown doctor hadn't passed him on the trail. Maybe he had gone another way.

But Jim was too tired and stupified to care. To hell with little fat strangers. Let 'em all get shot. He was too tired to answer questions or retaliate to rude remarks about his face. Finally the boys took pity on him and let him sleep.

He slept fitfully. When he awoke the room was full of sun shine. The rest of the bunks were empty. He felt horrible. This was much worse than the worst hang-over he had ever experienced. The light almost blinded him, but when he closed his eyes again the agony was intensified, the blackness was shot with sparks and searing flames. His head was a huge battleground, his body a boiling cauldron. He was on fire and shot to pieces.

He opened his eyes again. 'Greasy,' the cook, was carrying a tray across the room towards him. On it was a steaming mug of coffee, but no food. Only a bowl of water, piping hot, and rolls of bandage and cottonwool.

Jim scowled at the cook's grin and cheery greeting. Cursing softly under his breath at each twinge of pain, he drew himself into a sitting position.

'Better let me fix yuh up now, Jim,' said Greasy. 'You wouldn't let me touch you at all last night.'

'All right,' grunted Jim resignedly. 'But gimme that coffee first.' He reached hungrily for it.

After he had gulped it down he let Greasy do his damndest. He suffered like a martyr and, between curses at the fat cook's clumsiness, answered the usually taciturn Greasy's numerous questions.

After he had finished Greasy said 'Gosh, I'd shore like tuh see that Callahan this mawnin'.'

Jim, who now looked like the victim of a crazy barber, swathed as he was from the waist upwards in lengths of bandage, cottonwool, and sticking-plaster, grinned painfully.

'Yeh, I guess it wuz worth it,' he said . . . 'how's the old man this mornin'?'

'Oh, he's ravin' tuh go,' said Greasy. 'He wants to get up but your Maw won't let him. The wounded man who Jonathon picked up is still unconscious though. One of the boys rode into town to tell the doc to come early.'

'Yeh, I've a vague recollection of hearin' about a wounded man last night,' said Jim. 'Anybody know who he is?'

'Nope.'

'I'll go in an' have a look at him after breakfast.'

'You sit right thar, Jim,' said Greasy. 'I'll bring your breakfast into yuh.'

Jim shrugged. 'All right,' he said.

He ate a hearty breakfast with much puffing and muttered curses at his aching jaw and puffed tender lips. But he was so hungry mere pain could not quell his huge appetite.

After he had mopped up his plate and gulped down another cup of coffee, so hot it scalded his broken lips, he lit a cigarette and, leaning back, inhaled luxuriously.

He smoked two cigarettes and felt much better. He swung his feet out and down gently to the boards. He straightened up. He was still mighty stiff but that would pass.

He made tracks for the ranch-house and went upstairs to see his Dad. The old man was alone, propped up in bed, looking old and harmless.

'How yuh feelin', Dad?'

'I'm all right,' growled the old man. 'As soon as that pesky doctor gets here I'm gonna get up.'

Jim did not argue with him.

Pat continued: 'They tell me yuh've bin fightin'.'

'Yeh.'

'Callahan?'

'Yeh.'

'Did yuh beat him?'

'Yes, I beat him.'

'Good,' said the old man. His fire was dimmed, he seemed drowsy. He said: 'Your Maw's in the other room with that wounded stranger Jonathon picked up.'

'I'll go in an' have a look at this stranger,' said Jim. He found his mother sitting beside the bed. The stranger lay on his back, his plump stomach making a mound in the bedclothes.

'Hi-yuh, Maw,' said Jim and went nearer to the bed. He started when he saw the unconscious man's face. 'Gosh, it's Doc Rankin!'

'Yuh know him, Jim?' Surprise was in Beulah Lannigan's face and voice.

'Yeh, he useter to be doctor at Marlborough Junction. I met him when I was over there once.' Jim did not go into details.

'Have yuh got any idea what brought him over here. Or who shot him?'

98

'He was probably coming here because I told him to call on us any time he was in the part o' the country. I haven't any idea who shot him or why he was shot. Have all the men bin questioned?'

'Abel questioned most of 'em. Nobody seems to know anythin'?'

'And Jonathon didn't see anythin'?'

'No, he just found him there.'

'Tell me more about him, Jim,' said Beulah.

Jim did not want to tell her too much yet. In fact, he hadn't told anybody about his very narrow escape from having his neck stretched. Luckily at this juncture there came a knock on the bedroom door.

'Come in,' said Beulah.

Doctor Millership entered. 'Ah, good morning Mrs Lannigan,' he said. 'Good morning Jim. Where is this mysterious new patient? That is he. Ah!' Then, like Jim, he started. 'Why it's the little doctor I met last night. He was on his way to visit you, Jim.'

'I thought as much,' said the young man. 'Did he tell you anythin' else?'

'No, I didn't stay with him. I hurried on to attend your father.'

He crossed to the bed and drew back the covers. 'Ah, yes, the side, I see it has been bandaged.'

'Yeh, Abel Cornford done it,' said Beulah. 'He stopped the blood but I think the slug's still in there.'

'We shall see,' said the doctor. 'Pass me my bag, Jim. Mrs Lannigan, would you get me some hot water, please.'

'Right, doc.' Beulah left the room.

Jim handed the doctor his bag. 'Do you know anythin' about this, Doc?'

For a moment Millership looked shocked. 'Me? Why should I, Jim? I only met the man once. To tell the truth, I wondered what had happened to him that night. He shouldn't have been very long behind me.'

'It's queer you didn't meet Jonathon bringing him in

when you wuz on your way back to Jumptown.'

'I went another way,' replied the doctor. He was rummaging in his bag and finally he brought forth a shiny scalpel the sight of which made Jim shudder.

The doctor looked up. 'How do you feel after your combat of last night?' he said.

'Not so bad, thanks, doc.'

'I compliment you on your prowess.'

'Thanks.'

Beulah returned with a steaming bowl of hot water. 'Will yuh let me know when he regains consciousness?' Jim said.

'When I remove the bullet the shock should bring him round,' said Millership. 'Just as the shock knocked him out,' he explained.

'I'll hang around,' said Jim and he left them to it.

As he crossed by the corral a horseman came galloping up. It was Mick Lucas, the Circle Star's ace bronc-buster.

'Howdy, Jim,' he called cheerily. 'How yuh feelin'?' Everybody seemed concerned about him, reflected Jim sardonically. He tried hard not to feel gratified.

'All right,' he said. 'What you dashin' about fer?'

'I'm lookin' fer Crouch O'Brien,' replied Mick. 'Have yuh seen him?'

'Nope.'

'Wal, nobody's seen him then. He's no place on the range. He wasn't on night-guard last night, but all the same his bunk hadn't been slept in.'

'He didn't get knocked out an' left behind at the M.L.G. place maybe?'

'Naw. I've seen him myself since then. Early last night I seen him. Nobody seems to've seen him since tho'.' Mick dismounted. 'Anyway, Abel asked me to try an' find him so I might as well have a looksee hereabouts.' He grinned and made a bee-line for the cook-house. Jim followed him.

Greasy Masters, although he grunted irritably, brewed Mick the coffee he demanded. Although he still felt

100

bloated from his heavy breakfast, Jim had a couple of cups himself just to be companionable.

Greasy hadn't seen Crouch either and didn't partic'lerly want to. He turned away and began to bang utensils about and curse under his breath for no apparent reason – his usual reaction any time he was interrupted whilst at work in his kitchen.

The two cowboys took their time over their coffee and stayed to have a smoke also. The kitchen became full of smoke.

Finally Greasy turned on them with the irate request of would they 'get tuh hell away from him.'

Laughing and shrugging the two men left the kitchen but once outside they became sober again as they skirted the buildings in search of Crouch.

Jim did not know what to think about the disappearance of the misshapen little ranny. So bad were things becoming that he wouldn't be surprised to find Crouch's body lying around some place.

All was quiet around the ranch-buildings except for muffled clankings and bumpings issuing at intervals from the cookhouse, where Greasy was still in the process of 'cleaning up, after his visitors' smoky untidiness. Everybody else was out on the range. The quietness around the buildings was made up of the myriad hum of summer insect life. An unnoticed hum that was more somnolent than dead silence.

Passing around the back of the ranch-house proper the two men paused a moment and doffed their hats before the fresh graves of Clem and Bessie Lannigan. And Jim, at least, once more made a silent vow.

They went from the outside to the inside of the buildings with no success. Still no Crouch O'Brien!

'Wal, it looks like the ugly little cuss has plumb vanished,' said Mick Lucas. 'I guess I'd better ride back to Abel an' tell him.'

'It suttinly is a mystery where he could've got to,' said

Jim. He pondered with brows knit. He was stumped.

Just then his mother called him from the veranda. He bade *adios* to Mick and ran across the yard and up the steps.

'The little fat man's come to,' she said.

Jim followed her up the stairs.

Doc Rankin was still lying on his back, his blue eyes staring at the ceiling, his face white but quite composed. His eyes found Jim as the young man entered the room, and he smiled.

Jim wrung the plump hand that lay on the top of the counterpane. 'How yuh feelin', Doc?' he said.

'Not too bad, younker, thanks.'

'Have yuh got any idea who shot yuh?'

'Nary a glimmer. The slug hit me an' that's all I remembered.'

'Winchester repeater,' said Doctor Benjamin Millership, who had been washing his hands in the corner. He held out a bullet in the palm of his hand.

Jim took it and scrutinised it dubiously. 'Lots o' folks use these,' he said.

He looked down again at the man in the bed.

'What brought you here so soon, Doc? Have yuh got anythin' tuh tell me?'

'Not partic'ler, Jim. I jest came along 'cos you'd invited me. Yuh see, Hank Meltzer an' his men got a bit awkward. He's a mighty powerful man in the community is Hank Meltzer. I wuz gettin' tired o' Marlborough Junction – too much graftin' goin' on – so I decided to pack up an' seek pastures new.'

'I shouldn't talk any more now, doctor,' Millership broke in.

Jim was disappointed that Rankin could not tell him more, but he thoughtfully turned away.

Millership said, 'I'll come and see you again tomorrow, doctor. You know what to do.'

'Yeh, thanks a heap, Doc,' replied Rankin.

Jim said, 'I'll call in again after you've had a snooze, Doc. Keep happy. *Adios.*'

'*Adios*,' said the little man.

Then Jim left.

CHAPTER FOURTEEN

As he descended the veranda steps he saw a rider dismount from his horse by the corral. A little man in black with a bulging portfolio under his arm. At first Jim could not place him. Then he remembered: it was that cocky little lawyer who had called on his Dad some time back with Walt Eckerton. The M.L.G. legal representative or whatever he called himself.

The little man began to cross the yard to the ranch-house. As he got nearer he saw Jim. He made a jerky salute with his hand and said:

'Good morning.'

'Mornin'.'

'Where can I find Mr Pat Lannigan?'

'Wal, right now he's in bed,' said Jim. 'Somebody took a potshot at him.'

'I'm very sorry to hear that.'

'Are yuh?'

'But if I could possibly see him I have a message that I think will be to his advantage. My name is J. Woolington Scott. My – er – card.'

He held out the pasteboard. Jim ignored it. He felt mean. He said: 'I've seen you before. You're one o' the M.L.G. mob.'

This time he got the little man on the raw. He literally bounced as he said:

'Mob! I resent the M.L.G. Cattle Combine being referred to as a mob.'

Jim sighed and shrugged. 'Do yuh?' he said. 'Wal, I guess it's all a matter of opinion.' He stepped aside – back on to the veranda. 'You'd better sit out here while I get to know if the old man'll see yuh.' He motioned Scott to a wickerwork chair.

Old Pat received the news quite calmly.

'Bring him up, Jim,' he said. 'An' come in with him. See what you think about this mighty message of his.'

'All right.' The old man was certainly opening out since he stopped one. Not without amusement Jim wondered whether the wound had sent him temporarily soft in the head.

He ushered J. Woolington Scott into the bedroom. 'Good morning, Mr Lannigan,' said the little lawyer breezily. Then, without waiting for an answering greeting – which probably was not forthcoming, anyway – he continued 'I heard of your unfortunate mishap' – a snort from Pat, but no words – 'I hope you are feeling better now.'

'State your business, mister,' said the old man. He scowled as Scott drew a chair up to the bedside and sat down. J. Woolington was not a backward boy. Jim slouched against the closed door. His lips quirked as he watched the little pantomime.

The lawyer placed his bulging portfolio on the edge of the bed while old Pat watched him balefully. The lawyer unfastened the portfolio and brought forth a sheaf of miscellaneous shaped papers. He rummaged amongst these, strewing them about the bed. Old Pat's expression was murderous. He was obviously controlling himself with difficulty. Jim was hard put to control his mirth.

'Ah!' said the lawyer finally, and brought forth a folded yellow document. He wet his fingers quickly, professionally, and opened the paper wide with a flick and a crackle.

'Would you like to read that, Mr Lannigan?' he said.

Pat opened his mouth to say something, thought better

105

of it and with a grunt, took the paper. With this in one big horny hand he turned and thrust the other one beneath his pillow. From here he brought forth a spectacle case. The spectacles produced therefrom were steel-rimmed, very old, with cotton wrapped around the bridge. Pat scowled at the lawyer, then placed the spectacles on his beaky nose and squinted at the paper. His lips moved as he read laboriously. His head wagged slowly from side to side.

J. Woolington Scott watched him with bird-like interest. Jim lounged and looked disinterested, but inwardly he was alert. What kind of a trick were the M.L.G. trying to pull now?

The room was quiet for a moment then, suddenly, old Pat snorted violently. He turned savagely on J. Woolington Scott.

'Why, yuh pesky skunk, this is a bill of sale for all my land and holdings!'

'Quite so,' said the little lawyer unabashed. 'Although as I pointed out once before, my clients know that you have no legal right to the land they are willing to be magnanimous and buy it from you,' he smiled frostily. 'A nice little nest-egg on which to retire in your old age, Mr Lannigan.'

Jim could hardly believe his ears when he heard his Dad say quite mildly:

'They haven't filled in how much.'

The lawyer beamed. 'It is for you to name *your* price, Mr Lannigan.'

'Five million dollars,' said old Pat promptly. Jim grinned. Trust the old man every time!

Scott spluttered a little before he got his words out.

'Why, that's preposterous! You're making fun of me.'

'That's my price,' said Pat, blandly.

The lawyer took the paper from Pat's hand and stuffed it hurriedly into the portfolio. He fastened the portfolio and put it on the floor beside him.

'I should think it over, Mr Lannigan,' he said. Then

primly, 'Now before I go I have one more thing to tell you.'

'Shoot,' said Pat harshly. 'An' make it fast.'

'My news may be of interest to you – and it may not. I . . .'

'Let's hear it.'

But J. Woolington Scott was not easily intimidated. He said: 'I gather you are not very friendly with Mr Mancy Carter. Therefore, you may be gratified to know that he is leaving the M.L.G. Combine. He has given a month's notice. His place will be taken by a well-known Western character. I haven't met him personally but I am told he is quite notorious – one Steve Powley.'

'Marshal Steve Powley?'

'Ex-Marshal Steve Powley,' Scott corrected him primly.

'The man who cleaned up Hellcat Valley?'

' The cleaning-up of – er – Hellcat Valley was, I believe, one of his notable exploits.'

'D'yuh mean to tell me,' Pat almost bawled, 'that Marshal Steve Powley has gone over to that gang of dry-gulching robbers?'

Scott almost knocked his chair over as he rose swiftly. He certainly was a fiery little gent. 'I will not stay here any longer and hear my clients and – indirectly – myself, insulted in this manner.'

'Then git out, yuh pesky little pipsqueak,' bawled old Pat. He turned swiftly and reached under his pillow, bringing forth a Colt revolver which he waved at the infuriated little lawyer. Not to be outdone, Scott waved his fist in return, spluttering wordlessly as he backed to the door.

'I've a good mind tuh drill yuh . . .'

'Dad,' said Jim warningly, but grinning.

'Git!' Pat almost screamed.

J. Woolington Scott got. Jim closed the door gently behind him. Then he turned back to his Dad.

Pat was muttering under his breath as he returned the gun to its hiding-place under the pillow.

He looked at Jim and spoke aloud but it was as if he said it to himself.

'Old Steve Powley ramroding thet nest of robbers and murderers. We wuz kids together.' It seemed to Jim he had never seen the old man so concerned about anything – even the murder of his own son. He was disgusted again. His father was an unnatural cuss. Almost mad maybe. One day maybe he'd crack altogether.

Suddenly Pat's eyes blazed. 'See thet little skunk gets off the grounds pronto,' he said.

Jim shrugged and left the room. He could have stayed where he was – when he reached the yard J. Woolington Scott and his horse were a swiftly diminishing blob out on the range.

He returned. 'He's gone,' he said.

Pat's head was sunk on his chest. He merely grunted. Jim left and went along the passage to the spare room. His mother had gone and Doc Rankin was sleeping peacefully. There was more colour in his face and he looked plump and healthy. Nice little guy, reflected Jim. He must have a long talk with him later. It should be quite interesting. He owed the Doc a heap too. He had saved his life. And landed himself in trouble through his risky and unselfish action. And had to leave Marlborough Junction to boot. Jim wondered if one of the vengeful Waggon Wheel bunch had followed the little man here and shot him. It was possible – but it hardly seemed probable somehow.

Jim went outside again. It was his intention to saddle his horse and ride out to find some of the boys. But he paused a moment while crossing the yard. It was close to dinner-time. He felt hungry again. What was the use of going out before dinner? It wasn't worth while. He might as well have his dinner and go a-riding afterwards. His stomach won. He changed the direction of his feet and made for the cookhouse.

Greasy turned a red, perspiring face towards him as he opened the kitchen door.

'What, you again!' he groaned. 'Cain't you quit pesterin' me?'

'Is dinner ready yet, Greasy?'

'Dinner,' snorted Greasy. 'You've only jest had your breakfast.'

'Your cookin's so delicious, Greasy, that I cain't keep away from it,' said Jim with a very serious look on his face.

Greasy snorted again, but he did not sound so mad (his horneryness was mainly a pose anyway) when he said. 'It'll be ready in about fifteen minutes. Now, git, before I muss your face up some more.' His hand closed threateningly over the handle of a frypan.

Jim had his eye on some shortcake that was cooling on the windowsill. Suddenly he darted forward, grabbed a piece and bolted, banging the door behind him. Greasy's infuriated bellow floated after him.

Twenty minutes later Jim had his dinner with a few more of the men who had been working near and could get back to the ranch for their meal.

After a smoke and a chat he went back to the ranch-house and upstairs. Doc Rankin was still sleeping. Jim was disappointed. However, he saddled his horse and rode out on to the range. He looked out for Abel Cornford to find out whether Crouch O'Brien had been found, or any reason was known to account for his sudden disappearance.

He discovered Abel, with Kim and Jonathon, and a bunch of the boys, riding herd on a frisky bunch of new beeves. They were cutting out those of them that still needed branding.

No, Crouch had not been found.

'There's only one place I kin think of that he might be at,' said Abel.

'Where's that?'

'Widder Plummer's place in Jumptown. It's quite likely he rode in there last night. None of the boys seem to have

109

seen him since sundown. If he was pie-eyed the widder 'ud give him a bed like a shot.'

'Do yuh want I should go there an' see?' said Jim.

'Please yourself.'

'All right. I'll go. Cain't do no harm.'

Jim crossed the range and took the trail to Jumptown.

It was when he was approaching the semi-circular outcrop of rocks, known to many as Satan's Teeth, about a mile from the town that he heard the shot. He reined-in his horse for a moment. The shot seemed to come from somewhere just beyond Satan's Teeth – the echo was deceptive. He kneed his horse forward, drawing his gun, going warily.

He skirted Satan's Teeth and saw something before him half-concealed by the long grass. The white of an outstretched hand. The body of a man.

Jim dismounted from his horse and advanced. Slowly, gun in hand. He looked about him. Nothing in sight. The man lay on his stomach. Big, with dirty yellow hair. Familiar. A rapidly spreading red stain on his broad back. Jim holstered his gun. He grunted as he bent and turned the body over. Yes, it was Callahan all right!

He undid two buttons and put his hand inside the faded check skirt. The heart was still beating faintly, there was still a chance.

An alien sound, a mere undefinable something, made him turn swiftly, hand streaking to gun.

'Hold it, younker!' Jim froze. No good trying to draw against a Colt already levelled. Particularly when it was held in the hands of the cold-eyed Mancy Carter.

With Carter were three other men. Two of them were strangers to him. Something about the third struck a chord in Jim's memory. He was a big man and had a bushy black moustache. Jim realized with an inward start of surprise, that his fancy sombrero was minus a fancy band. Was this the mysterious hombre with the black moustache? It certainly looked that way.

110

The three men's guns were still in their holsters. That was something anyway. Jim kept his eyes on Carter.

Carter said 'Wal, yuh certainly didn't wait long to get back at Callahan. Shot him in the back like a yeller skunk. Good job we came along when we did.'

'Very neat,' sneered Jim. 'It might interest yuh tuh know that Callahan ain't dead yet though.'

Carter did not answer this. He seemed to be reflecting. His gun hand was still steady as a rock. Finally he said:

'Git your hoss. We'll take yuh both into town and get a doctor fer Callahan as quick as we can.'

Jim whistled his mount. The mare came trotting to him. He saw the line of her approach and became tense. For a split second Carter's line of fire was obscured by the mare's flank. Jim acted recklessly. Drawing, falling on one knee. One of the opposition was going for his own gun. Jim's first shot hit him in the shoulder, spinning him around. Then Carter came into view again. Jim swivelled his gun desperately as Carter fired. The slug hit Jim's gun, batting it from his hand, sending tingling agony the length of his arm. Some shooting!

'Nice play, younker,' said Carter. 'Bit it didn't work.'

'Nice shootin',' replied Jim. 'Very nice. It wouldn't suit your book to finish me off would it?'

Carter did not reply to this sally. His black-moustached companion walked round Jim and bent over Callahan. The other man went back to Satan's Teeth and returned with four horses. Nobody paid much attention to the fourth man who sat in the grass, nursing his shoulder with a hand through the fingers of which blood was trickling freely.

The black-moustached man straightened up. 'He's dead,' he announced.

'Everything comes to him who waits,' sneered Jim. 'You certainly fixed Callahan all right.'

Black moustache stepped forward and hit him savagely with his clenched fist. Jim went down, his face white, a red

111

patch where the blow had connected.

Black moustache kicked him, his eyes blazing. 'Get up,' he snarled. 'Get on that horse!'

Black moustache had certainly taken command with a vengeance. Jim eyed him murderously as he got to his feet. He climbed on his horse.

Black moustache turned to the others. He addressed the wounded man. 'Bart, you'd better ride back to the camp an' get that shoulder fixed. We'll take this young hellion into town.'

The man mounted and rode off. The other three mounted also, slinging the body over the front of the horse ridden by the wounded man's pard.

'Get moving, younker,' snarled black moustache. 'Any more funny moves an' I'll cripple you!' He certainly was a mad, vicious sort of cuss. For the moment Mancy Carter seemed to have taken a back seat in favour of him.

CHAPTER FIFTEEN

That night the arrest of Jim Lannigan for the murder of Callahan, the big Irishman, was the talk of Jumptown. Riding in search of him his four brothers soon learned of his whereabouts. He was in jail and heavily guarded while one particular section of the community planned a lynch-party.

The brothers moved among the crowds, most of them as usual in the Jolly Moses, and heard the whole story from friendly lips, while many not-so-friendly eyes watched them covertly. To see a Lannigan in jail was something over which to gloat. A bad breed – now was the chance to get rid of one of them. Callahan had fought the younker fair – and had got a slug in his back in repayment.

Callahan had been generous hail-fellow-well-met with the town's hangers-on and wild element. They would miss him. His cronies, many of them genuinely angry be it said, spread amongst them fostering the hatred, feeding the poison during round after round of drinks. Already a bunch of men were gathered on the boardwalk outside the Jolly Moses shouting and gesticulating wildly in the direction of the jail. The half-witted youth, 'Puffing Billy' was among them piping up from time to time to say that he had a 'nice leetle rope.'

They drew to one side as the batwings behind them swung open and Hannibal Lannigan and the others came through. Their talk ceased abruptly. Only poor, crazy

'Puffing Billy' gabbled on. Hannibal paused, his thumbs hooked in his belt, and looked at the boy. Then he looked around at the others. Nobody spoke.

Hannibal half-turned his head. 'C'mon,' he said. The other brothers followed him down the street.

'They're makin' fer the jail,' said one of the loungers. They jostled each other, getting into the Jolly Moses to tell the assembled company the news.

Sheriff Walt Eckerton lumbered clumsily to his feet as his office door crashed open. His deputy, Bison Jones, who suffered from rheumatism, was even less speedy. But the three shotgun guards with them already had their weapons levelled at the four Lannigan brothers. Jonathon was last. He closed the door gently behind him.

'Evenin', Walt,' said Hannibal, then he looked at the three guards. 'No need tuh look so warlike, boys. We've jest come for a little pow-wow.'

'Evenin', boys,' said the sheriff. His little flabby-pouched eyes shifted wanly.

'Yuh cain't keep Jim in jail like this yuh know, Walt,' said Hannibal, still in the same conversational tone. 'Yuh know as well as I do thet he wouldn't shoot anybody in the back. You've only got the evidence of three lyin' strangers.'

Eckerton looked uneasy. He didn't like his very prominent role in this set-up. He had always liked young Jim. Best of the bunch ... still ... 'their evidence was purty straightforward, Hannibal,' he said. 'They caught him standin' over the body an' he drew on them. He got one o' their men in the shoulder before they disarmed him. I had to lock him up. I couldn't do nothin' else.'

'Ain't it occurred to you that it might be all a frame up?' said Kim.

'Wal,' Eckerton's fat face perspired: he looked ready to burst into tears.

'Whoever fixed this is suttinly going a long way tuh get Jim hanged,' said Hannibal. 'There's a lotta lynch-talk

114

goin' on down the street there.'

This little item of news did nothing towards restoring the sheriff's equilibrium. He looked at Hannibal, Kim, Ep and Jonathon. He looked at Bison Jones. He looked at the three guards who were now leaning against the wall with their shotguns beside them. He found no comfort in any of these faces.

'What d'yuh want me tuh do?' he said.

'Let Jim free,' replied Hannibal promptly.

'But I cain't do that, Hannibal. I cain't . . .'

'Then his blood be on your head,' said Hannibal.

The sheriff looked around again. One of the shotgun men spat a stream of tobacco juice on the floor. He and his pards did not relish facing a lynch mob.

When Hannibal drew two guns on them, they started, but kept their hands strictly immobile. The other Lannigans drew their guns too.

'Bolt that door, Jonathon,' ordered Hannibal. Jonathon did so. 'You, Walt! Bison! Get over by the wall with the others. Get their guns, Kim. An' the keys off Walt's belt . . . You cain't be blamed for this Walt. I thought maybe we wouldn't hafta do it. It wasn't planned.'

Eckerton and his deputy obeyed Hannibal's orders with alacrity. The former seemed relieved that the initiative had been taken out of his hands. Kim took the keys and opened the door leading into the jail. They heard him walking down the passage.

A moment later he returned accompanied by Jim who saluted his brothers gravely. He helped himself to two guns.

'Lie down on your backs,' Hannibal said to the disarmed men. He waved his gun impatiently. They complied, Eckerton so hurriedly that his huge bulk shook the office.

'Now truss 'em up an' gag 'em,' said Hannibal 'Wait a minute . . . you,' he pointed to one of the shotgun guards. 'Gimme that coat an' hat.'

The man divested himself of these garments and handed them over and then in his turn had to submit to the far from gentle treatment of Ep and Kim who trussed his hands with his own belt and gagged him with his own kerchief.

'Put these on, Jim, an' take one o' the shotguns,' Hannibal said. He turned to Jonathon. 'How's it look out there?' Jonathon unbolted the door and opened it a crack. 'It's still quiet this end o' the street,' he said. 'But they're still millin' around by the Jolly Moses.'

'Probably waitin' tuh see if we pull anythin',' said Hannibal grimly. He turned once more to Jim. 'There's a spare hoss back o' Jeb Crockett's stables. You'll pass as a guard fixed up like that an' you won't have tuh go near the Jolly Moses. Watch your step. Get back home pronto!'

'How about you?'

'We'll be all right. We'll go out jest like we came in. We'll be right behind yuh. We'll be well away by the time anybody gets here. It's jest wind so far down the street there.'

Jim still looked dubious. At this juncture Hannibal's attention was drawn to sheriff Eckerton who was wagging his head from side to side and making faces. Hannibal crossed to him. 'If you shout, Walt, I'll blow your brains out,' he said. He removed the gag and bent nearer. The sheriff whispered in his ear. Hannibal nodded and replaced the gag. Then he returned to Jim and said something in a low voice.

Jim took the shot-gun in the crook of his arm and opened the door boldly. He stepped on to the boardwalk, tensed, but outwardly nonchalant, getting his eyes accustomed to the darkness. Then he looked about him. There was nobody near but, in the light that streamed from the Jolly Moses, he could see the men who milled on the boardwalk outside. They had been watching the sheriff's office and had spotted him. They did not move forward, however. So far it seemed Hannibal's little ruse had worked. The sheriff had whispered to Hannibal that there were three more shotgun guards round the back of the jail. Pretty white of old Walt, Jim reflected.

He could not go back along the street and round the back to the livery-stables for fear of being spotted by the guards. He must walk the other way towards the Jolly Moses and up the alley beside Jeb Crockett's place. It was not far. But he had to walk towards that hostile bunch who watched. So much could happen in those few yards that separated him from the alley.

His mind raced. But to hesitate too long would surely give him away. He began to walk briskly towards his goal. To his horror he saw two men detach themselves from the bunch by the Jolly Moses. He fondled the shotgun nervously – if they spotted him he'd start blasting. But they were coming along slowly, idly. Jim reached the alley and began to run. He hoped they couldn't hear the thud of his feet. The ground, however, was soft and deadened the sound.

He reached the top, turned the corner. The horse was tied to a post outside the Crockett's kitchen door. Jim mounted and without delay unhitched the beast and rapped him smartly with his heels. The horse set off. He was a fast beast.

Jim felt like a cur running out like this. He hoped his brothers would get away safely. He pressed the horse to its utmost; he knew what to do when he got home; his night was far from over yet.

As soon as he arrived at the ranch house he ran upstairs. Luckily his mother was not about to ask awkward questions. She was not in Doc Rankin's room, and the little man lay wide awake. 'You seem in an almighty hurry, son,' he said.

'I am,' said Jim. 'An' I ain't got time to explain why right now. I jest want to ask you a few questions.'

The Doc was shrewd. 'Shoot, son,' he said.

Jim thanked his stars for such a patient man. He said

'Yuh know Hank Meltzer who ramrods the Waggon Wheel. . . ?'

'I ought to,' said the Doc, smiling wryly. 'Now you are wastin' time. That's a fool question.'

'Sorry,' said Jim and smiled back. The Doc was a soothing influence.

Jim continued 'Wal, anyway, has Meltzer got a younger brother who looks like him?'

'He has,' said Doc Rankin. 'Young Pete Meltzer. Twenty-odd he is. He left the Waggon Wheel about twelve months ago an' nobody's seen him since.'

'Did he leave on his lonesome?'

'No, his pard went with him. A crooked-back hombre named Ike O'Day.'

'Here we call him 'Crouch' O'Brien,' said Jim. 'An' we useter call Pete Meltzer 'Corny' Macintosh. He got killed not so long back.'

'Yuh mean tuh tell me,' said the doctor, not quite so calmly, 'that them two have bin here.'

'They worked here,' Jim told him. 'Crouch – Ike O'Day or whatever you would call him – only disappeared last night. I figure it was him who bushwhacked you so you wouldn't give him away.'

'So he's bin up to no good.'

'It suttinly appears so, Doc,' said Jim rising. 'Thanks for the information. I think I know where I can find Crouch. I'm goin' after him now.'

In the passage he bumped into his mother. There was no need to avoid her now anyway.

'Jim,' she said. 'Where've yuh been. Where's your brothers?'

'I've bin in town, Maw. They're comin'. They'll be here soon. When they come tell 'em I'm goin' back to town and tuh get as many of the boys together as they can an' come in after me as quick as possible!'

Beulah saw his urgency. She realized her youngest was maybe the toughest and cleverest of the clan. He knew

118

what he was about.

'I'll tell 'em, son,' she said.

'All right.' And Jim was gone.

He was bound for the Widow Plummer's in Jumptown where he hoped to find Crouch O'Brien and make him talk. He did not want to meet his brothers, or the posse that by now might be following them, so he left the usual trail and made a wide detour that would take him alongside Old Smoky gulch. It was a longer trail, but, in the circumstances, the best he could do.

He was nearing the edge of the dried gulch when he heard the approaching horsemen. Quite a bunch by the sound of them. That was queer: it couldn't be a posse. Not coming in that direction. Why, they seemed to be coming right out of the Gila!

Luckily he was near the tortuous trail that led into the depths of Old Smoky. He eased his horse down here, and, leaving him, crawled back to the top. He removed his hat and peered cautiously over the rim of the gulch.

The horsemen, quite a small army of them, swept by, veering, heading across Circle Star range. Their faces were entirely covered by black cloth masks.

Jim let them get out of earshot, then fetched his horse to the top. His trip to town was definitely off. He rode back towards the ranch.

When he was almost there he ran into his four brothers. He did not waste time in congratulating them.

'The rustlers are raidin' again,' he panted. 'Jonathon, you ride on to the ranch an' rouse the men. It looks like they're makin' for the big herd. If the rest of us ride back there pronto we'll be able to help the night-riders hold 'em off till the rest get there.'

Jonathon was already on his way. The others turned and galloped off.

They heard the shooting before they reached the big herd. Luckily there was an extra strong force of night-riders there. Evidently they were holding their own for the time being.

119

The rustlers were on this side. The brothers, guns blazing, swept down on their rear. They broke and scattered, taken by surprise. The four swept through them bawling at the stop of their voices, fearful of being shot at by their own men. Somebody bawled in response: 'Hold it. It's some o' the boys.' The others sent up a cheer.

The two parties joined up as the rustlers, on seeing they had been spooked by only four cowboys, attacked again. The defenders were outnumbered three to one. The only way they could hope to survive was by keeping on the move, drawing the others on, playing for time.

Jim cursed as he saw one of the boys fall from his horse and lie writhing on the grass. He fired savagely at two oncoming horsemen and had the satisfaction of seeing one horse crash to the ground and roll on top of its rider. His companion fired and Jim's hat was whisked from his head. Someone was triggering methodically beside Jim. The oncoming rider pitched from his mount and fell on his face. Jim turned his head and received a sardonic grin from brother Kim. Then the stentorian voice of Hannibal heartened them as he bawled:

'They're comin'. The boys are comin'.'

And coming they were: a small army of them. And seeing them the rustlers turned and fled.

But as they fled the cattle were on the move. They were the most important item and frenzied Circle Star men let the rustlers get clean away while they tried to head off the suicidal mass of bovine flesh.

Dust was churned beneath flying hooves, faster, faster and the air was filled with thunder. To get in front of the mad charge would be suicide for horse and rider. They galloped alongside the leaders trying to turn them, slow them down, one fear in the mind of every man: the fear of Old Smoky. At the rate the cattle were travelling they would soon cover the mile or so to the yawning gulch. And if they kept on in that direction only one thing could happen.

Half-blinded by dust the horsemen risked broken limbs for themselves and their mounts as they travelled side by side with frenzied long-horns. Horses' flank pressed to steers' flank as the horsemen pushed, trying to move the almost mechanical mass over, over. The middle section broke a little but the leaders kept on: a hundred or so of them running like a single-minded mass. And following the dictatorship of mass mania the others instinctively changed their direction once more, trampling each other in their crazy eagerness. The horsemen had to veer their mounts frantically to avoid being knocked down. One luckless cowboy who had ridden too near the spearhead of the charge was bowled over. He fell clear of the cattle, but was almost stunned by the flailing hoof of a horse ridden by one of his own pards. He climbed to his feet.

Jim, Hannibal, Ep, Kim, Jonathon and Abel Cornford had stayed behind with the wounded and killed.

Two of the Circle Star men were done for. Also two of the rustlers. Three of the Circle Star men had flesh wounds.

It was Hannibal who spotted the man staggering towards them. Coming back from the direction the raiders had taken in their flight. He ran towards him, caught him as he fell.

'The skunks,' the man croaked. 'They left me.'

'Your boss,' said Hannibal. 'Who's your boss?'

The man coughed and went limp. Hannibal lowered him to the ground. There was one rustler who wouldn't raid other people's cattle any more. Pity he had not lived to say more.

The others came and clustered round the dead man.

'Know him?' said Hannibal.

Nobody did. 'Thet gang must be pretty heartless to leave a wounded man behind like thet,' said Jonathon.

'Whoever it is who leads them, he's ruthless and clever,' said Jim.

'This *hombre* cain't tell us anythin' now, but I know

121

somebody who will if we can get hold of him . . . an' don't forget I'm still wanted for murder. We've gotta work fast.'

'We're with yuh, Jim, in whatever yuh want tuh do.' Hannibal told him. The others spoke up in agreement.

CHAPTER SIXTEEN

Widow Plummer was a tiny ugly middle-aged woman with a club-foot, who kept the small honky-tonk right at the end of the main street of Jumptown, almost on the eerie slopes of Boot Hill. She ran a gaming table, sold liquor and had a few girls working for her. The men came to her place to play, to drink, and to 'spark' the girls. Widow Plummer kept pretty much in the background. Her late husband had been deaf and dumb. Since he died no other man had taken much notice of her. That is – until Crouch O'Brien came along. Their deformities seemed to draw them together. The widow was older than Crouch by twelve years or more. There was no 'sparking' about their relationship. They were almost like mother and son.

Every night he was in town Crouch spent in the Widow Plummer's, playing cards or, most likely, having a quiet drinking bout with the proprietress. After Corny Macintosh got killed Crouch spent a lot more time with the widow and got drunk more often. He didn't need money now. The widow would give him all he wanted without that.

This last time his sojourn at the widow's was lasting longer than ever. For a night and a day he had lolled on the cot in the back room, emptying bottle after bottle of whisky. The widow knew better than to ask him questions, but she was concerned about him. This second night he did not seem inclined to go either. He was hiding from

123

somebody: that was pretty obvious by now. And he was scared. He had drunk himself into a stupor. He couldn't look after himself now, so the widow guarded him jealously. Nobody else saw into that little back room.

But the widow could not be in the back with Crouch all the time. She had to appear out front now and then if only to allay suspicion. When she finally closed for the night, sending her employees home and locking up after them, she finally had the place to herself, she sighed with relief.

She returned to the back room and a stifled scream broke from her lips as she discovered that Crouch O'Brien was not now alone.

'Take it easy, Mrs Plummer,' said Hannibal Lannigan. He took her arm and guided her to a chair. 'Jest sit there an' keep your trap shut, an' you won't get hurt. You'll maybe make it easier for Crouch here, too.'

The widow kept silent and watched them with horror-stricken eyes. These Lannigan boys were a wild bunch: there was no knowing what they might do.

Young Jim, unshaven, unwashed, his face swollen and scarred and festooned here and there with strips of dirty sticking-plaster, looked an awesome sight as he bent over Crouch. The widow winced as the young hellion struck her favourite twice viciously across the face with his open hand. Crouch's head hit the wall against which the bunk stood. His lips drooled. He was helpless with drink.

'We're wastin' time,' Jim snarled. 'Get some water.'

Jonathon left the room. He returned with a slopping pail full of water. Jim took it from him, stood back a little, and slung all its contents with all his force at the drunken man's face. Crouch went down flat on the bunk and lay floundering and spluttering like a landed fish.

Jim caught hold of him forcibly by the front of his shirt and hauled him to a sitting position. He hit him again with an open palm across the side of his face.

'Crouch,' he said. 'It's me – Jim Lannigan.'

124

Crouch spluttered and wiped water from his face with the sleeve of his shirt.

'Jim,' he said. 'Whadyuh want?'

'We're all here,' said Jim. 'Look around yuh. Hannibal, Kim, Ep, Jonathon. We mean business. You know what we want as well as we do, and if we don't get it it'll be jest too bad for you ... an' maybe for Mrs Plummer, too,' he added darkly.

'I don't know what yuh're talkin' about,' said O'Brien.

'We haven't got much time,' said Jim. 'Doc Rankin's very much alive – you bungled the job, Crouch – or Ike O'Day, or whatever you call yourself. The Doc's told me all about you, an' about your pard, Pete Meltzer – Corny we called him – an' his big brother, Hank. Yuh see, we know a lot more than you think, Crouch. An' you know a lot too much. Enough to make somebody else want you right out o' the way. They killed Callahan yesterday, Crouch. You'd better tell us all yuh know or the same might happen tuh you. But if you come clean you'll only get a jail-sentence for plugging the Doc. That's better than a slug in the back, ain't it?'

O'Brien was cold sober now: the same, sullen, bitter Crouch of old. 'You're bluffing,' he sneered.

'Bluffin' am I?' hissed Jim. He jerked Crouch to his feet and thrust his battered face close to his. 'I've got too much at stake to let a little skunk like you stand in my way. Bluffin' am I?' His eyes blazed demonically as he drew back his fist and crashed it into the other man's face. At that moment he looked worse than his terrible Pa had ever done. Widow Plummer moaned and fell from her chair in a dead faint.

Jim dragged the bleeding man to his feet again and, swivelling him around, gave him a tremendous shove. Hannibal caught him and held him.

Jim took out his gun. He looked terrible but inwardly he felt slightly sick. His sudden passion had subsided. He didn't like what he was doing. But the thought that he was

125

dealing with a filthy bushwhacker and of how much was at stake made him harden his heart again. He balanced the gun in his hand.

'Ever bin pistol-whipped, Crouch?' he said.

The other man did not answer. Jim jerked his thumb at the inert body of Widow Plummer.

'After I've cut you tuh ribbons I'm gonna get to work on the old lady,' he said. 'Are yuh gonna talk?'

Still Crouch did not answer. His eyes glowed murderously. Suddenly Hannibal whipped a kerchief over his head, pulling it tight between his teeth, tying it at the back. Crouch tried to curse and couldn't.

Hannibal propelled him forward towards Jim. Jim's face was a white mask on which wounds glowed dully as he slashed Crouch across the face with the barrel of the revolver. A cry of agony, half stifled by the gag, burst from the man's lips.

'You cain't yell very loud with that in your mouth, Crouch,' snarled Jim. 'Nobody'll hear yuh. Are yuh gonna talk?'

The man was on his knees, his face covered with blood. He nodded his head.

Jim inaudibly sighed with relief. He was not cut out for this sort of thing. He helped Crouch to his feet and jerked the gag from his mouth. He menaced him with the gun. 'If yuh call out I'll finish yuh!' he said.

Crouch's eyes smouldered, but he had evidently made up his mind. He knew now that the Lannigans were not bluffing. He sat on the bunk. The five men gathered round him. There was no hope for it.

'Start at the beginning,' said Jim. 'The murder of Bull Kinsell.'

'Corny did that under orders from Joe Haffer,' said Crouch. 'He was to have what money he could get. Haffer wanted everythin' blamed on the M.L.G. That was part of his plan.'

'Haffer owns the Waggon Wheel don't he?' A big *hombre*

with a bush, black moustache.'

'Yeh, that's him. He's a maniac. It was all his idea. He sent me an' Corny on to get the lay o' the land an' wait for orders.'

'I suppose he already knew about the proposed M.L.G. ranch?'

'Yeh, Mancy Carter let him know all about that. They had worked the same game in different parts of the country. All the rustled cattle went to the Waggon Wheel and was rebranded.'

'An' I suppose the rustlers came from the Waggon Wheel – along the old Gila trail.'

'Yeh.'

'Who killed Corny Macintosh?'

'Joe Haffer I guess, he was there that night. Corny was getting scared an' drinkin' too much. He wasn't safe. Haffer probably told Hank that Corny had been killed by one of the M.L.G. men in a brawl.'

'Who was responsible for the murder of Clem an' Bessie?'

'Haffer I guess, it was like his handiwork. I had no part in any o' that, boys – honest.' Crouch looked around him at the hard, set faces. For once he seemed genuine. 'After Corny waz killed I wanted to draw back. But I couldn't. Haffer would've had me killed without turnin' a hair. He's a maniac I tell yuh!'

'Did any of the M.L.G. men – apart from Carter I mean – know about the rustlers?'

'Only Callahan I think. I know Pete Listery didn't. Callahan rode with them once or twice but he wasn't much good. An' he shouted and bragged too much.'

'I suppose that's why Haffer had *him* done away with too.'

'They say you did it.'

'Wal, I didn't,' said Jim. 'I guess you knew that.'

'Yeh. I guess Haffer did that too.'

'Mr Joe Haffer's certainly got some reckonin' comin' to

him,' said Jim. 'Maybe if he hadn't killed so many people he wouldn't have given us any clue. Apart from this it was a very simple and neat little scheme. An' the M.L.G. was the scapegoat all the time. Have yuh got anythin' else tuh tell us, Crouch.'

'No – I don't think so.'

'An' would you be willin' tuh tell sheriff Eckerton all you've told us.'

'I guess so. Now I've spilled the beans I guess I'd be safer in jail – with Haffer still on the loose.'

'He won't be loose much longer,' said Jim grimly. He turned to Jonathon. 'If the sheriff's back from scourin' the countryside lookin' fer me, bring him here.'

The leaders of the crazy, stampeding cattle plunged over the lip of Old Smoky. Two of the horsemen, over-zealous, only just escaped a like fate as their horses reared on the brink of the chasm.

There was nothing any of them could do. They drew away in a bunch, fearful of being forced over themselves by the maddened steers, and stood watching the crazy animals plunge to their death. Rank after rank, bawling, fear-crazed, vanished from sight in the yawning blackness.

But those behind were slowing down. Their senses told them all was not right. They smelled blood. They began to turn.

The waiting rannies seized their opportunity and rode forward, beginning to haze them away from danger as only men who understood them could do.

But almost half of the huge herd had gone over into the depths of Old Smoky. Another blow for old Pat. He was indeed, ill-starred lately.

Led by Abel Cornford they hazed the cattle back to their home-range.

Abel left a sizeable bunch of the boys with the herd, and, accompanied by the rest, rode back to the Circle Star to break the news to Pat.

The old man was out of bed and stamping up and down the corridor. Beulah barred the top of the stairs.

'You cain't go down,' she said. 'The boys are out. They'll look after things. You cain't do nothin' in your condition. You ain't as young an' tough as you useter be. Best make yourself contended an' get back intuh bed.'

'Make myself contented,' screamed Pat. 'While durned rustlers are running off my cattle. Get out of my way.' He swore at her, but she remained adamant. He did not attempt to get past her. He knew full well that, as he was now, she would be too strong for him. He didn't want to be handled like a child and bundled back into bed.

He continued to stamp up and down the passage, venting his spleen in childlike rage, kidding himself that he felt fine, although his head was spinning and his knees felt wobbly. He knew that if he didn't get back into bed soon he would collapse. But still he kept on.

Then Able Cornford came upstairs and Pat turned on him. What had he done? What happened? What was he standing there for?

'You'd better get back intuh bed, Pat,' said Abel quietly. 'I've got somethin' tuh tell yuh. It ain't good news, but it might've bin worse.'

'Get back intuh bed!' bawled Pat. 'Everybody tells me tuh get back into bed. Whadyuh think I am, a durned invalid?' He staggered. Abel and Beulah ran to him.

'Get away from me,' he screamed. He steadied himself against the wall, glaring at Abel. 'If you've got somethin' tuh tell me, don't stand there like a wooden Indian. Spill it!'

There was only one thing to do with Pat when he was like this. Give it to him straight.

Abel said: 'We drove the rustlers off. Killed two of 'em. But the shootin' started a stampede. Nearly half o' the big herd went over the edge of Old Smoky. We did our best. Tom Benson an' Whitey Franks were kilt. . .' but Pat had heard enough. He had gone quiet. Abel shut up, watching him. The old man turned and began to walk to his room. At the doorway he staggered, held the door-post. He slid to the ground. Abel and Beulah ran to him. He was unconscious. His wound had opened again and was bleeding freely. They carried him to the bed.

CHAPTER SEVENTEEN

Jim Lannigan had never before seen such a vision of radiant loveliness. Of women he had little experience. The young women he knew he could count on the fingers of one hand. In appearance none of them could hold a candle to this lovely creature. He was inarticulate as he gaped, feeling awkward, painfully aware that, with his face newly plastered by Greasy Masters, he definitely did not look his best.

Tall and shapely in riding kit. A heart-shaped face crowned by long golden hair atop of which was a ridiculous little prairie bowler worn as only a lovely woman could wear it. A-ah. And then the vision smiled, and the cool morning air seemed full of music and singing birds . . . Jim had hardly noticed the vision's companion until the man spoke.

'Good morning. By the looks of you I should say you were definitely a Lannigan. You look jest like your Paw did when he was a younker.'

Jim came back to earth and turned his foolish gaze on the speaker, an oldish, well-preserved tough-looking *hombre* whose lined face must have once been very handsome, whose blue eyes were still very keen. He could not be anybody but the girl's father.

'G-good mornin',' said Jim.

The visitors were very early. He was alone in the yard. He wished with all his heart that somebody else had been

131

there to greet them. Or at least that he had had some warning. 'I'm Jim Lannigan,' he added, feeling like a kid in short pants.

The old man wrung Lannigan's hand in his.

'I'm Steve Powley, a very old friend o' your Paw's,' he said. 'This is my daughter, Joyce. She's jest returned from school back East to settle down with her old man.'

Dreamlike, Jim, found himself grasping a cool white hand while another set of blue eyes appraised him coolly. Jim was doubly conscious of his battle-scarred face as he felt a crimson tide rapidly cover it from his neck to the roots of his hair. It was the first time he could remember blushing, but this fact detracted little from his discomfort.

'H-howdy,' he said. 'Miss!' He now felt like an ignorant clod.

'How d'you do,' she answered, coldly (or was that maybe his imagination).

'How's your Paw?' said Steve Powley.

Jim got a grip on himself once more. 'Wal, right now he's purty sick,' he said. 'I guess he's sleepin'.'

'We only arrived in last night,' said Powley. 'We heard of his ruckus with the M.L.G. an' how he'd bin wounded, but not much more. I thought he wuz gettin' fit again.'

'He was,' said Jim. Briefly he told, slurring over the more terrible facts, the story of the preceding night.

'An' Pat still blames the M.L.G. for everythin',' said Powley.

'I guess so,' said Jim. 'We haven't had a chance to tell him all the real facts yet.'

'Does he know I'm the new boss of the M.L.G.?'

'Yeh.'

'An' what's he think about it?'

'I guess he don't know what to think. I guess he's jest kinda puzzled.'

'I've allus bin a cowhand at heart,' said Powley. 'The buildings are nearly finished, an' when they are we'll get cattle in. I hope to make a first-class ranch there. There's land enough here for plenty o' people – even nesters. I hope your Paw'll realize that. Maybe when he's well an' I can have a straight talk to him like we useter I can make him understand.'

'I hope so,' said Jim.

'Perhaps it'll help if he knows Mancy Carter is lighting-out today.'

'Today!' burst out Jim.

'Yeh, he wuz packin' when we came away.'

At this sudden piece of news Jim forgot his nice manners. 'Perhaps you'd better see Maw,' he said, and almost ran them to the ranch-house. He ushered them into the front room, fetched the half-mystified Beulah and then left the house as if all Satan's minions were on his tail.

His brothers and many others were already up.

'Have the sheriff an' his men arrived?' said Hannibal.

'No . . .'

'The fat, lazy skunk!'

'Steve Powley's here. He says Mancy Carter's leaving,' said Jim, buckling on his gunbelt. 'I'm going after him.'

He was on his way. 'You cain't go alone,' said Hannibal.

'Then foller me,' yelled Jim impatiently over his shoulder. As he ran to the stables he heard Hannibal bawling at the others.

Maybe Carter smelled a rat! If he did he wasn't to be allowed to get away and warn his pals at the Waggon Wheel. He had to be stopped!

As he rode out he looked back once. His four brothers were running out of the bunkhouse. Hannibal shouted but he paid no heed to him.

When he was about half-a-mile from the M.L.G. camp he began to make a detour. He didn't want to ride right in and get picked off by the rifle of a guard. Although he was boiling to be face to face with Carter he realized that only by craft could he attain that end. Maybe the man had already lit out. He hoped to gosh he hadn't!

He rode until he was below a rise which he figured roughly faced one side of the camp. Just there they weren't so likely to have a lookout. He breasted the rise slowly, and reined in his horse.

The camp lay just below him at the bottom of the slope. Jim was surprised at the progress that had been made since he had seen it last. Which wasn't so very long ago at that! It was beginning to look something like a ranch now. And what a ranch! A cattleman's dream!

Somebody was standing on the edge there looking at the horseman. Jim cursed and went back behind the cover of the rise. He rode along a little further, waited awhile, his ears alert for the sound of approaching horses. All seemed quiet. Perhaps the watcher had taken him for a wandering saddle-tramp and was not in the least suspicious.

He breasted the rise again and looked down at one of the rear corners of the camp. A deserted corner it seemed. He began to ease his horse gently down the slope.

The M.L.G. workers strove with a mighty will. Their task was nearly finished. Then, as was their custom, there would be a gigantic booze-up in the nearest town, in this case, Jumptown, before they set out for pastures new. Too bad big Callahan wasn't with them any more. He was always the boyo for a spree. There was a rumour about now that that young Lannigan feller hadn't killed him after all. What the hell! They would soon be leaving this country for good. It had been exciting while it lasted. Many were the philosophic shrugs, or the bovine grunts and gestures. And they forgot Callahan.

There was a rumour that ex-Marshal Steve Powley was coming to take over the ranch itself. It was a fact – some of the fellers had seen him with Carter last night. He was almost a legendary figure in the West – the others hoped they'd see him too before they left.

And Mancy Carter – there was a rumour that he was leaving them for good. But not Pete Listery. Listery was mild and tractable, his querulous temper a mere pose. They could handle him. They even had a sneaking regard for the little man. But *that* Carter! They wouldn't be sorry to see him go. He was a hard one!

The object of their thoughts was sitting by the cold stove in his cabin, smoking a cheroot and contemplating the future with a complacent half-smile on his hard face.

His bulging bed-roll, his war-bag, his slicker, his rifle, lay against the wall beside him. His hat was on the back of his head, his boots spurred, his loaded gunbelt around his waist, his well-oiled guns fitting snugly in their holsters. He had always been coldly methodical. He was ready to go.

No hurry though. Time for a quiet smoke, reverie: no regrets and rosy dreams for the future. He'd taken a chance all his life. What he'd got now he'd earned by his wits and his guns. Lesser men had gone down before him. He owned only one boss, and he a madman who he would soon leave in the past too. It was time he settled down. A ranch, a saloon, maybe a wife, in a place where nobody would bother him.

He leaned back in his chair, its two front legs off the floor, his one foot on the cold stove, blowing smoke rings to the roof. A sudden knock on the door made him start. He righted the chair, his feet banging down on the boards.

'Come in,' he snarled. They couldn't leave a man alone! What the hell was that commotion out there?

The door opened and one of the workers entered.

'The sheriff and his men are here, boss,' he said. 'They're after you. Listery's talkin' to 'em.'

Carter was startled. What had happened? Had somebody talked? His mind raced. Crouch O'Brien! Yes, if anybody had talked it could only be him.

He turned to the gaping man: 'Get my horse!'he snapped. 'Quickly, man.'

The man bolted. Carter drew his gun, opened the door again and looked out. So far all was clear. For a moment he was irresolute. Perhaps it was only a minor thing

135

Eckerton wanted to see him about. But he'd brought his men with him. No use taking chances. He didn't mean to wait and risk sticking his neck into a noose. He was going anyway. Why the hell didn't that man hurry up? Where had he got to?

He looked out again. The voices seemed to be coming nearer. Then he saw the man with his horse.

'Hurry,' he said. He was almost panicky as he ran back into the cabin to get his things.

'They're comin', boss,' yelled the man.

Too late now, he must leave his stuff. He grabbed his rifle and ran out again. As he mounted he saw sheriff Eckerton and Hannibal Lannigan. Behind them more men.

'Carter!' yelled Hannibal. He had a gun in his hand.

Carter put spurs to his horse. Hannibal fired. Carter felt the wind of the slug. Then he skirted an outhouse which shielded him for a bit. As yet his pursuers were unmounted. He had a chance. He urged his horse forward to the back of the camp. A few men here stared at him curiously. Nobody got in his way. Beyond – the open range and freedom! The horse cleared a barrow with a leap as he spurred it cruelly.

A worker said something and got in his way. Carter waved his gun at him. There was murder in his face. The man wilted, turned and ran.

Carter was nearly out in the open when another horseman came round the corner of a disused toolshed and towards him. Carter fired point-blank. As horse and rider rolled in the dust he realized it was Jim Lannigan. He laughed harshly as he spurred for the open range.

CHAPTER EIGHTEEN

Joyce Powley had spent three years in a young ladies' academy back East. An untutored man himself, her father set great store by book-learning for the younger generation. He had hung up his guns and only now carried a small pocket-derringer for security. There were plenty men in the West who still owed Marshal Steve Powley a grudge.

While his daughter was away Steve lived quietly in different parts of the West where he was not so notorious (he could not bring himself to leave it altogether), learning to be a gentleman. He did not realize that men like him were the 'first gentlemen' of their land. Their kind were dying out now, but their deeds would never be forgotten.

Joyce knew her Dad wanted her to be 'a lady', but if some of the simpering, catty, men-chasing hussies she had met back East were ladies, she decided she would rather be a simple backwoods girl. Despite this she did very well in her studies – and promptly forgot most of them.

In her eyes the Eastern men were even worse than the women. Tailor's dummies with none of the old-world courtesy practiced by Westerners to their women-folk. Lady-killers, tennis-players, dancers – with minds either like cess-pools or complete vacuums.

She followed her Dad's wishes and stayed her full three years. But many was the time she was tempted to catch a train and go back to the West to stay. She longed for its hills, its mountains, its boundless plains, its heat in summer, its Northers in winter, its cool breezes at night and its skies that seemed the bluest, with stars the most sparkling. The short vacations she spent with her Dad only served to make her longing more poignant.

Now, at last, she was home to stay, home in Arizona, her Dad's own country, back to make her home on a ranch of the sort she had dreamed about. She was eighteen. Sometimes she thought she should like to marry some clean young cowboy with the West in his blood, as it was in her own. To settle down with him in a little homestead. To cook for him, sew for him, raise his children. To be a real Western woman like her own dimly remembered mother had been.

Jim Lannigan was the first man of her own generation she had met since she arrived back in the West. Despite his battered visage, he had affected her favourably, more so as it was evident her own appearance had smitten him more than somewhat. He was such a tall, well-built young man, a typical Westerner, something clean and untamed about him. He had evidently been fighting. Joyce was not at all taken aback – hadn't her father once earned his living by fighting? She only wondered why he had been fighting. And whether he had won or not.

When he suddenly terminated their interview, handing them over brusquely to his mother and leaving without as much as a 'so-long' she was piqued even more.

Beulah received the visitors civilly enough, but was almost as brusque as her son. Very independent sort of people these Lannigans! She had met Steve Powley a few times before. He was a very old friend of Pat's. This was in his favour. However, they could not see the old man. He was still sleeping. He was worn out. She didn't know whether he would want to see his old boyhood friend – in the circumstances . . .

She herself was not so prejudiced against the M.L.G. people. She knew now that they had not been responsible

138

for the rustling and killing. But still they had no business settling on people's land like this without as much as by your leave.

'They don't know you and your husband and your circumstances,' said Steve Powley gently. 'They don't know how you fought and toiled for this land. The law's a funny thing, Mrs Lannigan, it sets a lot of store by bits o' paper: deeds an' sechlike things. When they asked me to run their new ranch for 'em I talked to that little pipsqueak of a lawyer, J. Woolington Scott, and he told me where it was and how the owner of the neighbouring ranch who laid claim to the land was a stubborn ol' goat who wouldn't sell.'

Beulah snorted.

'After further enquiries I learned the exact situation of the new ranch and realized the old goat in question was none other than my old pard, Pat Lannigan.' Steve grinned. Beulah tried hard to look stern. She couldn't manage it. She smiled thinly.

'Wal, knowing Pat, I guessed the M.L.G. people were goin' about things the wrong way. Fancy offering to buy him out. That little worm, Scott, didn't realize how near he got to havin' his pompous backside filled full o' lead.' Steve paused to chortle. 'The little rat was quite indignant at the way he'd been treated . . . still, I suppose he was only trying to do his job. His bosses sitting back there in their offices were really to blame for everything.

'Wal, I had a pow-wow with a few o' these bosses. I explained to 'em that under old Western laws, the law that Pat, and I, if it comes to that, had lived by and couldn't be expected to give up at this stage of our lives, all the Smoky Range territory belonged to the Circle Star.'

Steve paused again. Beulah was looking quite interested and expectant. Joyce was sitting at the window looking out to the range, drinking it all in, making up for three years of bondage – although her Dad did not suspect this. He continued:

'Finally they agreed on a scheme to pay rent to Pat for the land they're using. I know he won't give it up altogether. I've got to admit, seeing the law is as it is, it's a purty generous gesture on their part. An' as far as they're concerned Pat's cattle can graze with theirs. All the land'll be open as its always been. Only the brands'll be different. It'd almost be an amalgamation of the two ranches. Seein' as I'm gonna ramrod the other spread I thought maybe Pat'd consider it. I'd strongly advise it. By law he ain't got a leg to stand on. Yuh see what I mean, don't yuh, Mrs Lannigan.' Steve was very earnest.

'Yeh, I guess so,' said Beulah. She pondered. 'It surely was a big blow losing all them cattle last night, I guess this scheme'd sort of help us along. It don't seem bad to me. I guess the two of us can get Pat around to our way of thinkin'.'

Steve beamed. 'Good fer you, Mrs Lannigan.' Then he became grave again. 'We only got in last night. I heard you'd had trouble but I didn't know how bad it was.'

Beulah told him the whole story. When she divulged that Mancy Carter was one of the leaders of the rustlers Steve was startled and shocked.

'If we'd known when we were talking to him this morning,' he said.

'I didn't know till just now,' said Beulah. 'The sheriff and the boys've gone after him.'

'So that was what young Jim was so het-up about,' said Steve.

'Yeh,' said Beulah harshly. 'The crazy young fool went after him on his lonesome. The others are trying to catch him up.'

Joyce was listening now. So Jim Lannigan was riding into danger. She found herself praying that he would come through safely. She heard her father saying:

'Wal, from what I saw of Jim, I guess he's a match for Mancy Carter.'

'Yeh, but Carter's got pals,' said Beulah. Her hardness

140

was a cloak to hide her worry. She dreaded losing another son. For years she had schooled herself to toughness, but lately her hard shell was beginning to crack. She couldn't do anything about this. She didn't know if she wanted to.

'Don't you worry, Mrs Lannigan,' said Steve. 'Jim'll be all right.' He couldn't think of anything else to say.

'Of course he will, Mrs Lannigan,' said Joyce. Was it only her fancy or did her voice quaver a little?

Hannibal cursed and lowered his gun. Carter was hidden by one of the numerous toolsheds that cluttered the camp. Walt Eckerton was puffing and blowing beside him. Hannibal realized the fat sheriff was too much out of breath to give an order. So he gave it himself.

'Get your hosses,' he bawled, and began to run back, shepherding the others before him.

'Get mine as well, Hannibal,' the sheriff wheezed, and stood rooted to the spot mopping his streaming face, with quite a few of the M.L.G. men watching him seriously. They had never seen a law-officer quite like this before. Then the sheriff was hidden as the clearing was swamped once more by horsemen. The Lannigan brothers, about thirty Circle Star men besides, and the sheriff's own size-able posse culled from the hard-riding, law-abiding element of Jumptown. Hannibal led the sheriff's mount.

With much grunting and puffing and a great air of martyrdom fat Walt clambered aboard. His horse was big and rawboned, and wore a perpetual bored expression. After carrying fifteen-stone Walt for so long the beast had ceased to be surprised at anything. All men were fools, and his fellow quadrupeds who carried less weightier mortals, were beneath his condescension.

'Let's get goin'!' shouted Hannibal.

The cavalcade moved forward. 'I thought I heard a shot,' said somebody . . . 'Yeh!' . . . 'An' me!' . . . Then they reached the outskirts and saw the tumbled horse and rider.

'It's Jim,' said Hannibal.

The horse lay with horrible staring eyes, its chest covered with thick blood. Hannibal dismounted and ran to his brother. Jim stirred and groaned.

'He's jest knocked-out,' said Hannibal 'The hoss stopped the slug.'

'Give him a shot o' this,' said Jonathon, and produced a flask from his hip-pocket.

Hannibal supported Jim in a sitting position. The young man's eyes fluttered open. 'Here, take a swig o' this.' Hannibal pressed the flask to his mouth.

Jim took a swig. He shook his head violently. Then he grinned and took the flask himself, taking another deep swig. 'I'm all right,' he said. 'I must've bin half-addled tuh start with tuh give that skunk a chance tuh throw down on me like that . . . where is he?'

'He got away.'

'Wal, what're we waitin' for?' Jim hauled himself to his feet. 'Let's get after him. It's a purty safe bet he's makin' fer the Waggon Wheel.' For the first time he seemed to notice his horse. 'Poor ol' gel. I guess she saved my life.' But time was being wasted. 'Get me another hoss, somebody,' he bawled.

One of the M.L.G. men, proving co-operative, brought forth a fast-looking bay. Jim removed the saddle from the dead horse and transferred it to the back of the other. He tightened the cinches quickly, expertly. He mounted.

'Let's ride,' he said.

The cavalcade swept out on to the range. Most of the M.L.G. men watched them go. Thing's certainly moved fast in this part of the country. Most of them hoped the posse would catch up with Mancy Carter and string him up on the highest tree they could find.

Instead of leading his posse Sheriff Eckerton soon found himself riding in its last ranks. The Lannigan brothers were well in front. Walt shrugged his fat shoulders. It wasn't his war anyway. He'd a good mind to turn back. But he knew he wouldn't. He was sheriff. His job was not too bad in ordinary times. Right now he'd just keep jogging along, grunting, cursing, and sweating, getting tired and saddlesore. And there was always the chance of stopping a bullet at the end of the ride. *Still, be was sheriff, wusn't he? What the hell. . . !*

The foremost members of the posse topped a slight rise. Before them the range stretched endlessly, mating with the sky in the purple infinite.

'There he is,' said Ep Lannigan, pointing.

He was a mere blob on the shimmering green immensity. He certainly had a good start. The pursuers swept on. Sheriff Walt Eckerton groaned aloud.

'Buck up, Walt,' said one of the posse. 'We've hardly started yet.'

The sun beat against them as if to drive them back. The grass was blue and shimmering beneath it. To look at it for long brought headaches and partial blindness. The men rode with their hatbrims pulled down low, their eyes squinted. The sweat ran down their faces in little rivulets. From time to time a man produced a water-canteen, newly filled at the M.L.G. camp and threw back his head to take a quick pull. Their faces were set and hard, they breathed through their noses. They were implacable. The man-hunt, the dreaded custom of the West, was in their blood.

CHAPTER NINETEEN

The sun was at its highest, beating down on them with scorching fury as they reached Jose's Joint. They were travel-stained, their eyes red-rimmed, their mouths dry, their faces caked with sweat and dirt. All the horses were lathered and beginning to blow. The men dismounted and led their mounts to the convenient water trough where they milled and snorted while they waited their turn to get a drink.

Then men filed into the cantina. Jose, flustered and perspiring, stood in the middle of his floor and beamed nervously. It had been years since he had so many customers all at once. His fat wife fluttered about in the shadow of the kitchen doorway.

Jose recognized the Lannigans. 'Ah,' he said. 'You return to my leetle place.'

'Yeh,' said Hannibal harshly. 'But we're in a hurry. Let's have some coffee as quick as you can!'

'Yes,' Jose turned and bawled at his wife who immediately vanished in the darkness beyond.

'Do you know Mancy Carter, Jose?' said Jim.

'A big dark man. He's been in once or twice with men from the Waggon Wheel. He has been in today – not more than half-an-hour ago.'

'He has!' echoed Jim. 'We're on the right track then, boys. He's headin fer the Waggon Wheel all right.'

While they were waiting for coffee they went outside,

144

group by group, to have a swill at the pump and refill their canteens. Jose bustled into the back to help his wife. A few moments later they came through again together, carrying a tray each, loaded with steaming cups of almost black coffee.

'Good work, Jose,' bawled Hannibal.

The trays were quickly emptied and the Mexican and his wife took them back. Pretty soon they returned again with the trays loaded once more. Four times this happened and then everybody had had at least one cup. Jose's eyes popped at the money that was piled on his counter by appreciative hands.

Everybody felt a whole heap better – even sheriff Walt was raring to go. There was no time to be lost. They mounted again and galloped out of Jose's yard in a cloud of sand.

Another hour's hard riding brought them into the Kyper Flats country, and Waggon Wheel territory. At a sign from Hannibal Lannigan they halted.

He stood up in his stirrups. 'Go slower, men!'he yelled. 'An' keep your eyes peeled. They probably know we're here by now.'

They cantered on. They saw no signs of human life. Plenty of cattle but seemingly no riders to guard them. Then the Waggon Wheel ranch-buildings came into view. And still not a soul in sight.

Hannibal halted his men just out of rifle range. He motioned to his brothers. 'Us five'll go forward,' he said, 'Fan out. Keep your eyes peeled.' There was no need to tell them this. They were alert as, singly, they left the others behind them. There was something ominous about the stillness of the Waggon Wheel ranch. Then a rifle-shot shattered the silence into a thousand echoes.

And with that shot began the battle of Kyper Flats. Nobody was hurt by the shot. The Lannigans wheeled their horses and returned to the others. Walt Eckerton had come to the front again.

145

'What d'yuh suggest we do, sheriff?' said Kim sardonically.

The sheriff blinked his little eyes and wished he had
stayed at the back.

'I guess we charge 'em,' he ventured.

A grizzled old-timer, known in Jumptown as Calamity
Gibbs, and reputed to have three dozen wound-scars on
different parts of his body, kneed his horse forward. He
was an old Civil War cavalry man.

'That's right, sheriff,' he said. 'A charge of cavalry 'ull
put the fear o' death into 'em. But we'll have tuh spread
out, a few yards between each man.'

'I guess you're right, Calamity,' said Hannibal. 'We'll
make it three lines. Right?'

'Right!' said Calamity. 'One wide charge – an jest
behind 'em two shorter lines to take each flank. Circle 'em
Injun fashion an' keepa-riding.'

'Everybody ready?' said Hannibal.

There was a chorus of 'ayes.'

By tacit agreement the Circle Star riders with the
Lannigans in the centre made up the first long line of
men. Sheriff Eckerton split his posse up into two
sections.

The first line began to move, slowly at first, then, as the
Lannigans began to set the pace, at rapidly-increasing
speed. Calamity Gibbs, who had insisted on riding with the
brothers, began to give vent to a piercing war-whoop. The
cry was taken up all along the line. Eyes flashed, teeth were
bared, heads thrown back as men screamed like savages
and spurred their horses to greater efforts.

As they got within range the defenders opened fire.
Calamity Gibbs screeched as a slug whipped his hat from
his head. He waved his revolver as if it were a sabre and
cursed the enemy at the pitch of his lungs.

Jim Lannigan winced as a slug nicked his shoulder.
Jonathon's horse neighed with pain as a slug creased its
ear. Only the fact that its rider was leaning in the saddle

146

saved him from getting the slug in his chest. As it was it only brushed his sleeve.

Along the line a horse screamed shrilly and fell to its knees. The rider was thrown clear. Another rider stopped a slug full in the face and fell from his saddle. His one foot was caught in the stirrup and his body was dragged along by the horse, who, with no burden on his back, drew in front of the others. Finally it shared the fate of its rider and, as a slug bored into its neck, screamed and went down, mangling the poor human body beneath it.

The fire was becoming withering. More men and horses went down. The line began to straggle. But by now Sheriff Eckerton's parties were coming around on each flank. Walt himself was bouncing along and yelling as loud as the next man.

The riders were all firing now. Lying across their horses' necks, showing as little of themselves as possible. Just a hand with a gun spitting flame. More than a few luckless beasts stopped a bullet intended for their masters. Eckerton's men were now skirting each side of the ranch buildings, many of them lying alongside their horses' flanks, Indian fashion, and firing across the beasts' backs.

The defenders were concentrating more now on the flanking movements. They obviously had a sizeable force in there, but also obviously lacked shooting space. Riding nearer on the flanks many riders saw them crowded at windows and were able to fire into their midst.

The Lannigans and their men were creeping up again and beginning to join the circling movement. Nobody was near enough to the back, however, to see the two horsemen who broke away from there and streaked away across the range. Pretty soon the horsemen were galloping all around the house. The defenders were hemmed in. They began to come out of the house, and stables, and bunk-houses, to dodge behind barrels and carts. Now it was too late many of them sought for an opening in the ranks of the attackers. The horsemen began to dismount and close

147

in on foot. Many a clash occurred in the yard.

Jim Lannigan threw himself from his horse facing the back of the house and ran for the cover of an upturned cart with one wheel. Out of the corner of his eye he saw Jonathon follow suit. Then he lost sight of him. He must have taken cover somewhere else.

A few yards to the right of Jim was an outhouse that looked deserted. He turned his eyes away from it and looked at the main buildings. A door opened and two men scuttled out, making for cover among the conglomeration of articles that littered the yard. Jim stepped out of cover, two guns levelled and blazing. One of the men went down. He never knew what hit him. The other fired back wildly, taken by surprise. Jim's second shot hit him in the shoulder, spinning him around.

'Look out, Jim,' somebody yelled, and as he half-turned a slug nicked the brim of Jim's hat. Jonathon was standing now between him and the outhouse, firing at the man who blocked its doorway.

Jonathon had never been a gunfighter. He had not trained like the others. His shot hit the door jamb. Then the other man retaliated and he went down.

Jim ran forward, firing across his brother's body. The man staggered away from the doorway, his hat falling from his head, the sun shining on golden locks. It was Hank Meltzer.

Jim fired again savagely. Meltzer fell forward on his face. As Jim ran to his brother the yard was filling with men. The battle was almost over. Men were coming out of the buildings with their hands above their heads.

Jim raised his brother's head. 'Thanks, Jim,' he said simply. He realized, now it was too late, how much he had misjudged his brother, the so-alien Lannigan. Jonathon's 'yellow streak' had been a caution the others lacked, his gentleness the courage of tolerance and idealism. Jonathon looked into his brother's eyes and smiled, a gentle smile that forgave all and had no regrets, a smile that would stay with Jim and ennoble him for the rest of his life.

Jonathon died as Kim dropped on his knees beside Jim. The latter shook himself as if from a trance. Then he rose, leaving Jonathon in Kim's arms and ran to Hank Meltzer who was moving feebly.

Jim pulled the big yellow-haired man up into a sitting position. His shirt was saturated with blood. He was pretty far gone but he recognized Jim and smiled crookedly.

'Where's Haffer and Carter, Meltzer?' Jim asked.

'They've gone,' replied the dying man. 'I should've been with 'em only I left things a bit too late . . . pity – they – they'd got all the money, too . . .'

'Where they headin' fer?'

Meltzer leered. Jim had to admire his guts. Even in death he was defiant. 'Wouldn't you – like to know?' he said.

Jim leaned nearer. 'Meltzer,' he said urgently. 'Listen to me. Haffer killed your young brother.'

'He – he was killed in a brawl,' said the man.

'Haffer killed him I tell yuh, Meltzer. He cut his throat. I wouldn't kid you now, Meltzer.' The man's eyes flickered. 'Tell me where they've gone, Meltzer. Tell me . . .' Jim bent closer. The man was trying to say something. The words came out in staccato phrases.

'Gila – right out – rock shaped like sombrero – smaller rock each side – green piece back there – camp – we cached more money there in case of accident – nobody else . . . Haffer knows desert . . . best go at night . . .'

Hannibal joined them. Meltzer's head fell back. Gently Jim lowered him to the ground. Hurriedly he told his elder brother what he had heard.

'We'll go together,' said Hannibal. 'Jest you an' me. One apiece.'

CHAPTER TWENTY

The desert was cooler now as the sun began to sink. The men had penetrated deeply into the fabulous no-man's land, seeking blindly, not knowing whether they were going in the right direction, but trying to keep in a straight line from where they entered the Gila at a point opposite the Waggon Wheel ranch. They looked into the sun-glare, seeking a rock shaped like a sombrero, until their eyes burned and tears ran down their cheeks. Soon it would be getting dusk and they would have to give up their quest, for one night at least.

Their faces were unshaven, dry and caked with dirt. Their teeth and gums were dry and gritty, their lips cracked, their eyes so leaden they had an almost overpowering desire to close them, but they had to keep them open, wide open, peering, in case they should miss something. They spoke little for words were difficult to articulate with throats that felt like shrivelled leather. They had only a canteen full of water apiece out of the four they had brought, so had to be sparing with drinks.

Jim was beginning to wonder whether Meltzer's tale might be nothing but the last defiant joke of a dying man. He wondered what Hannibal was thinking, but did not dare to ask.

The sun was nearly down. Shadows were beginning to creep across the dry, hard ground. A little chill breeze began to blow.

Jim strained his eyes, peering forward, his head aching

so much that he thought it would split. Then his lips opened, only a croak came from them, but his hand shot out and caught Hannibal's bicep in a grip that made him wince.

At last Jim got his words out.

'I can see it! There, look. Over to the right. We nearly missed it. I only spotted it out of the corner of my eyes.' The stolid Hannibal was almost as excited. He turned his head and looked for himself. 'Yeh, I see it. It looks like a sombrero. An' there's a littler rock each side of it. That seems to be the place all right.'

'We don't want to get too near in case they spot us.'

'If they're still there,' said Hannibal.

'Hell, I hope they are,' said Jim.

'In any case I guess it'd be safer to wait till dark before we cover the rest o' the ground. If they're there we don't want 'em to run out now.'

'Sure,' said Jim. He groaned as he slowly dismounted from his horse.

'Here, over here back o' these rocks,' said Hannibal. 'It's back o' the rise. If they're keepin' a lookout they're not likely to spot us here.'

They led their horses across. They unrolled their slickers and wrapping themselves in them sat down with their backs against the rocks. The Arizona nights, particularly out here in the desert, were in direct contrast to the days, just as cold as the days were hot, with little seeping winds that froze the marrow in a man's bones.

Both men took a pull at their canteens, then scratching a shallow depression in the hard-baked sand, tipped a drop in for the horses. It did not have time to drain away: the thirsty beasts licked it up, and every drop of moisture from the earth beneath it. Neither man spoke but brought forth their guns and saw that they were in first-class working order, well-oiled, the cylinders clicking rhythmically as they spun them.

The night fell swiftly, like a cold blanket. There was no

moon and the cold diamond-like stars were very high. Jim looked above the rock. He could still faintly see the sombrero rock. Even he had its direction: he knew he could ride straight to it.

Hannibal rose to his feet. 'I guess it's time we got started.' Jim followed suit. They mounted in silence and moved slowly forward.

Presently Jim said: 'We must be gettin' close now. I vote we leave the hosses an' go the rest o' the way on foot.' Hannibal grunted assent. They dismounted. Walking awkwardly, but silently, on the sand in their high-heeled boots, they got nearer.

'They're here,' hissed Jim. 'They've got a fire. See its glimmer between the rocks.'

'They must've bin pretty sure of not being found here.' whispered Hannibal. 'I guess they didn't think Meltzer 'ud give 'em away. I bet they're wonderin' where he is now.'

They could hear voices now. They reached the sombrero-like rock and crouched behind it. Then they realized the voices were raised in argument. They looked cautiously around the rock. It annoyed them to discover that yet another cluster of rocks lay between them and their quarry. The edges of these were tipped with crimson: the reflection from the fire beyond. The men sitting by the fire could not be seen but the other two could hear plainly what they said.

Jim recognized immediately the snarling tones of the black-moustached Joe Haffer. He was saying:

'There was more than this I tell yuh . . . Mancy, if you double-crossed me . . .'

Carter's voice was almost plaintive. 'You know me, Joe. How could it be me. I've bin too busy. An' I've bin with you a lot.' His voice became softer, took on a cunning note. 'How do I know it ain't you yourself? Maybe you're jest puttin' on a show now to pull the wool over my eyes.'

'When thieves fall out . . .' quoted Jim softly. Hannibal gripped his arm as Haffer bawled:

'Don't haze me, Mancy, yuh know it ain't me.'

'Don't yell, Joe . . . how do I know it ain't you?'

By contrast now Haffer's voice was a savage hiss. 'Wal, somebody's bin here. If it ain't me an' it ain't you, there's only one other person it can be.'

'Meltzer,' said Carter excitedly. 'It must be Meltzer. He oughta be here by now. Why ain't he here? It must be him.'

'It's easy to blame Meltzer,' said Haffer harshly, sardonically. 'When he gets here I guess he'll blame us . . . if he gets here.'

'I believe he won't,' said Carter. 'I believe he's grabbed as much as he can an' lit out someplace we can't find him: I bet he had plenty cached somewhere else, too. I ain't bin satisfied with the way he's bin actin' lately . . .'

'Well, why didn't yuh speak,' hissed Haffer.

'You're the boss. You seemed to be satisfied.'

'So I'm tuh blame all along am I,' snarled Haffer. 'You are a mighty man, Mancy . . .'

'I didn't mean that, Joe,' said Carter, now using a conciliatory tone. 'We've bin pards a long time. We . . .' he broke off suddenly. 'Joe, did yuh hear that?'

'What? I didn't hear nothin'.'

'I heard somethin'. Somebody's about, Joe.'

Haffer laughed. 'The wind. You're jumpy. You're hearing things.'

There was a sound of scraping boot-heels. Carter said: 'Perhaps it's Meltzer.'

Then he appeared round the corner of the cluster of rocks. The firelight glinted on the gun in his hand. His face was in darkness, but he seemed to be staring right at the sombrero-like rock behind which Hannibal and Jim were hiding.

A gun boomed behind him. Carter staggered forward a few steps as if he had been pushed. He half-turned, trying to bring his own weapon round: for a moment his face was etched by the firelight: contorted, surprised, terror-

153

stricken. Then the gun boomed again. Carter's body described a black-etched arc. The gun flew from his fingers. He fell flat on his back, rolled over, his legs working convulsively. Then a horrible choking cry came from him. A terrible cry of despair. And he lay still.

Haffer came round the rocks, his gun still in his hand.

'You poor fool, Mancy,' he said, and callously prodded the body with his boot.

Behind the sombrero rock Hannibal drew his gun. Jim caught his wrist. Haffer disappeared from sight again.

'Let me take him, Hannibal,' said Jim. 'I owe him more than you do.'

'We'll toss for it,' said Hannibal stolidly.

By the fire Haffer was talking softly to himself. Now and then he chuckled; little eerie blood-chilling sounds. Money jingled as he muttered and cackled.

Hannibal produced a coin. In the starlight they could just discern its markings. 'Call,' he said and spun it.

'Tails,' said Jim.

It landed silently in the sand. The two heads bent near it. Jim straightened up first. He gripped Hannibal's shoulder and jerked his other hand, thumb pointing out to the desert. Silently Hannibal rose. His huge bulk vanished in the darkness.

Gently Jim eased himself around the corner of the sombrero rock. He tiptoed across the intervening space and stood behind the cluster of rocks. Carter lay almost at his feet.

Jim looked round the rocks above the body.

Haffer was squatting on his haunches before the fire. At his side was a leather bag. On the sand in front of him was a pile of bills and coins, winking and glittering. Haffer was picking them up in handfuls and running them through his fingers. His face in the firelight was ruddy and contorted, his eyes shone, his lips writhed; he babbled words but Jim could not hear what they were.

His thumbs hooked in his belt, Jim stepped into the

clearing 'Hello, Joe,' he said.

Haffer sprang to his feet, leaping in front of his beloved money. His eyes blazed madly, he screamed curses. Then he went for his gun.

Jim drew swiftly, coolly, firing from the hip. Haffer's mouth opened in a scream as the heavy slug tore into his chest. He staggered back, back until he was behind the money. His gun, clenched in his hand, was out of its holster, but he hadn't had time to level it. His thumb pressed on the hammer. The slug buried itself in the ground. Then the gun dropped from nerveless fingers.

As Jim watched dispassionately, remembering Clem and Bessie and Jonathon, Haffer slowly sank to his knees. The money was before him: he was on his knees before it like a heathen worshipping at a shrine. As he sank lower his clawlike hands reached out, scratched at it, scrabbled deep grooves in the sand around it, as its worshipper struggled in his death throes. Then the lifeless body of Joe Haffer fell forward.

Mechanically, Jim holstered his gun. He strode forward and rolled the body away with his foot. He gathered the money together, and stuffed it into the leather bag. He carried the bag with him, leaving the bodies for the buzzards of the morning.

Hannibal was awaiting him by the horses. Solemnly the two brothers shook hands.

Father and daughter dismounted from their horses at the Circle Star corral. She looked boyish in a blue check shirt, a red kerchief at her strong brown throat. Her jeans were tucked into high-heeled riding boots, her golden hair almost hidden by a wide-brimmed grey Stetson. Only her face was wholly feminine, and startling in its beauty.

Her father was like a much larger masculine edition of herself. He wore no gunbelt, only a plain leather sash with a silver buckle.

A tall figure came towards them from the direction of

the cook-house. Joyce halted. Her father grinned and, with a wave of his hand, strode on to the ranch-house.

Jim reached Joyce and grinned down at her. Only a scar along his chin remained as a reminder of his battle with the late-lamented Callahan.

'I bet you've been pestering Greasy again,' said Joyce.

'He shouldn't make shortbread,' was the retort. Then Jim looked about him quickly and, bending over, kissed her. She clung to him for a moment. Then she drew away. 'Have you spoken to your Dad?' she said.

'Wal, no – not yet.'

'Oh, Jim, you promised.'

'But I'm going to as soon as your Dad's finished in there.'

Pat Lannigan looked up as his door opened. His leathery face relaxed a little as he saw who his visitor was.

'Mornin', Steve,' he said.

'Mornin', Pat. How are you this mornin'?'

Pat shrugged and grunted. He hated being fussed. He was deep in his favourite armchair. By his side rested his stick. It was just there in case one of those pesky doctors – there were two of them now, Millership and Rankin having gone into partnership – called suddenly. He didn't really need the durn' stick.

Steve Powley took a seat. 'Fine bunch o' steers we've got in the North pasture, Pat,' he said.

The older man grunted again. 'I ain't seen thet new batch yet. I'll hafta ride down there this afternoon.'

'Looks like we got some more 'nesters' on the edge o' the line,' said Steve.

Another grunt. Pat said: 'I've seen the time . . .' He finished the sentence with a shrug of his huge bowed shoulders.

Steve smiled. 'I guess we might have some more soon,' he said.

Jim Lannigan was crossing the yard towards the ranch-house as Steve descended the steps. Joyce was still standing by the corral. The two men passed.

Steve grinned. 'He's all yours, son,' he said.

When Jim opened the door his Dad was sitting with his leonine grey head bent, his chin sunk on his chest. He raised it slightly and looked at his son from under bushy brows. 'Ah . . . Jim,' he said.

The young man's face was set. 'I'd like to pow-wow a bit,' he said.

'Sit down, son.'

Jim remained standing. 'Joyce Powley an' I want to get married an' make a homestead of our own,' he said.

Pat looked up at him. He did not look at all surprised. His face relaxed, the nearest it got to a smile.

'Wal,' he grunted. 'If you've made your mind up tuh that, son, I guess I cain't do nothin' tuh stop yuh!'